Perilous ~~Adventures~~
of Sammy Squirrel

A children's fantasy

Steven J. Scott

MAPLE
PUBLISHERS

The Perilous Adventures of Sammy Squirrel

Author: Steven J. Scott

Copyright © Steven J. Scott (2023)

The right of Steven J. Scott to be identified as author of this work has been asserted by the author in accordance with section 77 and 78 of the Copyright, Designs and Patents Act 1988.

First Published in 2023

ISBN   978-1-915796-43-1 (Paperback)
         978-1-915796-44-8 (eBook)

Book cover design, Illustrations and Book layout by:

White Magic Studios
www.whitemagicstudios.co.uk

Published by:

Maple Publishers
Fairbourne Drive, Atterbury,
Milton Keynes,
MK10 9RG, UK
www.maplepublishers.com

Contents

Chapter 1: Bounder Keeps His Promise

Samuel T. Squirrel (known to everybody as 'Sammy') sat back in his favourite chair and lounged. He simply didn't have the energy to do any more squirrelling on this beautiful autumnal day, with the golden and copper leaves stacked up against the hedgerows.

Sammy had spent the last few weeks in hectic foraging, digging, and storing food for the winter. He'd skipped from tree to tree and fence to fence until he was thoroughly exhausted. Now that enough supplies had been stored up it was time to relax.

Mrs. Squirrel had just returned from collecting herbs, and was working on a wonderful hazelnut stew. The two youngsters, Slippy and his sister Snowy, were playing noisily outside, chasing each other around in circles, and through bushes and heather.

The small family of red squirrels lived in a long and winding drey in the suburbs of a large city. There were many oak, ash and chestnut trees, and some excellent hiding places for keeping food and avoiding wily and belligerent crows, who could get very nasty when in large groups.

Sammy had been dozing off in his chair when suddenly there was a very loud, insistent knocking on the front door.

"What is all this commotion?" cried Mrs. Squirrel.

"Don't worry," Sammy replied, "I'll see to it."

Sammy rose from his chair, and sleepily pushed the front door open. He was shocked to see his neighbours, Mr. and Mrs. Dibbs, two nervous-looking squirrels, looking even more worried and agitated than usual. "Oh Sammy!" squeaked Mrs. Dibbs in a high-pitched voice. "You must help us – it's that horrid stray cat called Scratch! He's got our children – Rusty and Pippy – trapped in a tree, and they can't escape!"

Sammy invited Mr. and Mrs. Dibbs to come in and sit down. "I'll brew some tea for us all," said Mrs. Squirrel, and she added a few twigs to the flame under her little tea-pot, mixed in some herbs, and sat opposite them.

"Now calm down, and tell me what happened," said Sammy, for poor Mrs. Dibbs was wringing her hands in anguish.

"They were playing on the other side of the road – I've told them repeatedly not to cross the road – it's too dangerous – but they won't listen, and now that wretched cat has chased them up a tree, and they are stuck there! Oh Sammy, what can we do?"

Sammy leaned back with his eyes closed, and his ears began to twitch (which they always did when he was thinking). Just as Mrs. Dibbs was becoming very impatient Sammy jumped up from his chair, opened the door, and called his children in. When they saw how serious their father looked, Slippy and Snowy thought they were about to be told off, and looked at each other sheepishly. "I have a very important job for you two," said Sammy, in a quiet, firm voice. "You must leave for Mr. McKinley's farm immediately. Hurry there and fetch the wolfhound, Bounder. Now, take this with you." Sammy started to rummage in a chest of drawers and finally, from the very bottom, he took out a battered and torn collar and passed it to Slippy. Slippy and Snowy looked at each other quizzically, and then back at their father.

"Don't worry," said Sammy. "Bounder will know what it means. He will follow you back and chase Scratch away. But you must leave – right now!"

Slippy tucked the collar deep into his coat pocket and turned to his sister, "Let's go – quickly!"

"Oh," said Mrs. Dibbs. "I do hope this will work. I'm so afraid of that awful cat!"

"It will work," Sammy spoke confidently. "Now, sit yourselves down and have some tea."

*

Slippy and Snowy wasted no time in scurrying off towards McKinley's farm. Now, in general, these young squirrels would never turn down the chance of an adventure – but this was different. To fetch a wolfhound from a farm inhabited by many dangerous creatures – not to mention farmer McKinley himself, was not their idea of an exciting adventure – it was far too risky. But this was an emergency, and when they thought of poor Rusty and Pippy trapped up in a tree, with Scratch just waiting for them to come down, they hurried on. They scampered along leafy lanes and across golden fields where horses grazed and birds pecked at the soil. As long as they had the collar they felt sure that Bounder would not harm them. However, dogs were large, unpredictable, and sometimes very fierce.

At the railway crossing they clambered over an old gate that led into the next field. Snowy was slowing down as they approached the farm.

"Slippy," she said in a small voice. "I'm frightened."

"We'll be fine. We have the collar." Slippy searched in his jacket pocket – and searched some more. "Oh no!" he gasped. "We've lost the collar – it's gone."

For a moment they were shocked into silence, their eyes round with horror as they stared at each other. But then Slippy recovered his wits. "There's no time to panic – we'll have to double back and find it! Quickly, Snowy – we must hurry!" And they raced away over the fields.

*

In the swaying branches of a gnarled old tree, two little squirrels were quivering with fear. There were no other trees nearby to leap to, and besides, Pippy had sprained her ankle as they had run up the tree to escape from Scratch. Beneath them the stray cat prowled silently, menacingly, and then sat down on a nearby tree-stump. "I can see you," said Scratch in a rich, smooth voice which sent shivers through the young squirrels. His eyes were cold, with cruel, narrow slits. "You can't stay up there forever, but I can wait ... I'm in no hurry." And he grinned up at them, licking his paws slowly and meticulously.

*

Sammy tried his best to sound calm. "They should be there by now," he assured Mr. and Mrs. Dibbs. "It shouldn't take them long to return with Bounder – don't worry – you'll soon have your children back." Mrs. Dibbs was still wringing her hands, and Mr. Dibbs did not reply. He was trying to be brave, but anxiety was making his heart beat faster and faster.

*

Slippy and Snowy were growing desperate. They could not find the missing collar. They had not dropped it in the fields or the paths they had crossed. They had all but given up when Slippy had an idea – "I know, maybe it fell out of my pocket when we climbed over the railway gate." They raced along until they came close to the railway tracks. "We will have to be careful," said Slippy. "Wait here while I take a look."

Slippy searched all around the area of the railway crossing, and was just about to leap onto the tracks when he heard a cool, sharp voice ring out.

"Don't move – stay where you are!" A second later Slippy felt a flow of hot air rushing past him as a huge locomotive roared past, only a tail's length from where he stood. He ducked and covered his ears as the train sped by. When the train had passed, Slippy lifted his head. He felt a new sensation of dread and fear as he saw who the voice belonged to. From the other side of the tracks, sitting quite still on top of a boulder, was a large russet-coloured fox.

"Is this what you were looking for?" asked the fox, his sharp bright eyes fixed on Slippy.

The fox picked something up from the ground and clutched it in his jaws. To Slippy's surprise he realised it was the collar they had been searching for! The fox placed the collar on the ground in front of him, and examined it carefully.

"Hmm, very interesting." In the blink of an eye the fox had crossed over the railway tracks and was sitting beside Slippy and Snowy. "You are Sammy's children, are you not?" This was more of a statement than a question, and Slippy could only nod in his terror. "I am called Felix. Stay away from the tracks – they are dangerous. Now, why were you searching for this?"

"Our father gave it to us – to fetch the wolfhound, Bounder." Slippy blurted out the story of the trapped squirrels and their attempt to save them. Felix pondered this for several moments. Finally, he nodded and pushed the collar towards them

"Very well, take the collar. And do not lose it again. Tell your father you saw me." Slippy was too scared to say any more, and Snowy had frozen on the spot, and seemed to be in some kind of daydream, but when Slippy nudged her awake, Felix had gone.

*

Sammy was worried. He knew something had gone wrong, but he didn't want to alarm Mr. and Mrs. Dibbs. He thought about going to fetch Bounder himself, but he knew he could never get there and back in time. Could he fight off Scratch on his own? If it came to it he would have to try. Sammy could move very quickly when he needed to, and perhaps he could outwit the cat, but just one swipe from those sharp claws ... he sat back in his chair trying to look relaxed. He would wait a little longer ...

*

Slippy and Snowy slowed down as they neared the farm. Through a small gap in the fence they could see that farmer McKinley was inside the farm house, and they could see Bounder resting by his kennel

9

outside, casually gnawing at a large bone. "He looks mighty ferocious," said Snowy.

"Yes," answered Slippy, his heart pounding. "But we must try to save Rusty and Pippy." And they climbed nimbly over the fence, and then stood staring at the immense bulk of Bounder as he turned his head towards them.

Bounder had had a rather dull week, and he was very bored. Farmer McKinley was pre-occupied, as his family was visiting, and the farmhands were much too busy to even notice Bounder. There was not much Bounder could do except rest and wait until the visitors were gone. He was just about to doze off again when he heard a scurrying sound, and when he turned around he couldn't believe his eyes. For standing in front of him were two very young, very frightened squirrels.

Slippy took the collar from his pocket and, trembling from head to foot, approached Bounder. When Bounder saw the collar, he stood up and a low growl issued from his throat. He looked formidable, and when he spoke his voice was deep and rough, and seemed to echo around the farm-yard.

"I have not seen this since ... you have been sent by your father?"

"Yessir," Slippy stammered, and he quickly explained why they had come. "So, you see, Mr. Bounder, we need your help to chase Scratch away and rescue Rusty and Pippy ..." When Bounder heard the name 'Scratch' another growl echoed around the yard.

"Show me where – and hurry – it will soon be dark."

*

Scratch was beginning to lose his patience with the two squirrels hiding in the tree-top, when suddenly he turned and was horrified to see the giant figure of Bounder the wolfhound hurtling towards him. Before turning to run he hissed up at the two squirrels. "You may have escaped this time, but I'll be watching." And he scrambled away rapidly, through an alleyway, with Bounder close behind him, barking and chasing for all he was worth.

"Come on down, quickly!" Slippy was half-way up the tree, calling out to Rusty and Pippy. The cat's gone."

"It's Pippy," Rusty answered. "She's hurt her leg." Just as Slippy was out of ideas Bounder re-appeared after his long chase after Scratch.

"He got away, but he won't be back for a while."

Slowly the young squirrels made their way down from the tree, but Pippy could barely walk on her injured leg. Rusty and Pippy were trembling at the sight of Bounder, but despite his gruffness Slippy could see a kindness in the large wolfhound's eyes. Bounder sat down next to Pippy. "Climb onto my back, and hold on tight," he told her. "I'll carry you home."

It did not take long to get back to their drey, but as the sun was going down Bounder looked up at the gathering clouds. "I'll leave you here. I must return before farmer McKinley notices I have gone. Tell your father I kept my promise – take good care, little squirrels." And with that Bounder turned and leapt away into the darkness.

*

While Mr. and Mrs. Dibbs were hugging their children in relief and joy at their safe return, and Snowy was being tucked up in bed by Mrs. Squirrel, Sammy took Slippy to one side.

"Now," said Sammy quietly, "tell me what happened." And he sat back with his eyes closed and listened as Slippy related their adventure. When Slippy had finished his tale, Sammy whispered to his son.

"You were very brave – you and Snowy. I'm proud of you both. But remember, you were very fortunate with the collar – if you'd have lost it ..."

Slippy nodded. "Bounder spoke of a promise ..."

"Yes, yes indeed. Many years ago, when Bounder was but a pup, he was captured and taken to a bad place where stray dogs were kept. I happened to be passing by on my travels and saw Bounder chained up by his collar outside. I couldn't help the other dogs, but I was able to bite through Bounder's collar and free him. He was very weak, but I managed to get him to McKinley's farm. Well, McKinley's wife took pity on Bounder and nursed him back to health. They kept him on as a guard-dog and he has been there ever since. Before I left, Bounder told me to keep the collar and gave me his promise that if I ever needed his help, to show him the collar and he would repay me for his freedom. He has honoured that promise today."

Slippy said nothing for a while, and then he asked:

"But how did Felix find it, and how did he know exactly when the train was coming? I didn't even hear it."

"Foxes know everything," Sammy replied, "and Felix is certainly one of the cleverest."

"But why did he help us – I thought we were done for!"

Sammy sat back again, and smiled at Slippy.

"Ah, Felix. Yes, well, that's another story."

*

Later that night Mrs. Squirrel spoke to Sammy. "Oh, I'm so relieved that Rusty and Pippy got back safely! Poor Mr. and Mrs. Dibbs were beside themselves with worry. Sammy, I don't feel very safe here anymore. The humans have cut down so many of the trees, and the road is too dangerous to cross now, and these wretched cats and crows ..."

Sammy's ears twitched. Before the family went to bed that night he called them all together to make an announcement.

"Mrs. Squirrel and I have decided it is time we left here. We will be moving into the Great Forest where it will be safer." Slippy and Snowy stood wide-eyed. Sammy continued. "We have cousins there who will welcome us, and there are no roads or human machines to worry about. So, get off to bed now, and tomorrow morning we will pack and leave – for our new home in the forest!"

Chapter 2. The Rickety Bridge

Early the next morning Snowy's tufted ears and dark brown eyes appeared above the entrance of the drey. She sniffed the air and hesitated. Then with a sudden burst of speed she raced up the nearest sycamore tree to have a look around.

It was dawn, and the early dew was on the grass. Her brother, Slippy, and her parents were still sleeping. But Snowy hadn't slept much, she was too excited – for this was the day the family were moving to make a new home in the forest. Foraging for food would be easier in the Great Forest, but far more exciting, was the thought of meeting their cousins, making new friends, and having a whole new world to explore!

The sun was beginning to rise as Snowy climbed, and she was about to leap to another branch when she heard a ruffle of wings above her, and lifting her head, looked straight into the calm golden eyes of a very large brown owl, who was observing her closely. She was unsure what to do – stay still, or try to leap to safety – when the owl spoke to her, in a rich, mellow voice. "Well, little squirrel, what might be your name?"

Snowy tried to hide her fear as the owl gazed steadily at her, and she replied boldly. "I'm called Snowy, and I live with my brother, Slippy, and my mother and father. He's called Sammy."

"Sammy Squirrel," said the owl, tapping a sharp curved talon on the branch beneath his feet. He blinked his eyes slowly, and began to stretch his wings. "Well, Snowy, I'm very glad to have met you. Tell your father that Bramble said 'hello'." And with that he quickly fluttered off, leaving Snowy feeling mightily relieved, and a little confused. She'd never met an owl before, but she'd been warned to stay away from them. She took another look around, but seeing nothing of great interest, she scampered back down the tree and into the drey, and closed the door tightly behind her.

Mrs. Squirrel was in a fix. She was trying to pack everything they needed for the journey to the forest, trying to rouse the children from their slumbers, and trying to cook breakfast – all at the same time. Sammy was doing his best to help, but seemed to be getting in her way more than he was helping, so she had ordered him out of the kitchen and told him to get on with his packing. Now, Sammy was much too smart to attempt to argue, so he made his way to the storage rooms to see how much food they would be able to carry with them.

Neither Sammy nor Mrs. Squirrel had noticed that Snowy had gone out and returned, but her brother Slippy knew she had wandered off and come back. "So, where have you been?" he asked Snowy.

"Oh, just outside for a bit," she replied.

"Did you see anyone?" he asked her suspiciously.

Snowy didn't reply, but looked down at her feet. Before Slippy could question her further, Mrs. Squirrel was glaring at them in her apron. "Breakfast is on the table," she snapped. "Now, go and find your father. After breakfast you can get your things packed – there's no time for loitering this morning!"

Sammy was counting the stores when Slippy and Snowy found him. "Breakfast is ready, dad," said Snowy.

For a moment Sammy looked at his children. Slippy was growing rapidly and would soon be able to look after himself – and Snowy – he grew fonder of her every day. She had been named Snowy for the long streaks of white in her tail, and the white patch on her forehead. Unlike her brother, she seemed to have stopped growing, and would remain very small. But she was incredibly fast, and by far the best climber and jumper of any of the young squirrels. She was very quick to learn, and she already knew where to find the best hazelnuts and pine cones, and the best hiding places for storing food.

Sammy was confident that the journey to the forest would not be too hazardous, and that with any luck the family would get there within a few days. Now it was time to eat, and then their new adventures could begin!

*

Bramble flew low over the fields. His outstretched wings beat in a leisurely fashion, and his sharp eyes surveyed the ground for careless prey. But Bramble was more tired than hungry. He had been hunting all night and was looking forward to returning to his roost – an old disused farm building on the edge of the forest.

Bramble was an owl of habit. He didn't often fly far from his roost, but this night, for some reason, he had wandered a little further afield, and had stopped to rest in a large sycamore tree before returning home. Here he had caught sight of a very young, curious squirrel on the branch below him. Bramble lived alone, and rarely spoke to other creatures, partly because he preferred to keep his own company, but also because many other creatures feared him. But this little squirrel was different. The strange white streak in her tail, and the way she spoke to him without fear, instead of trying to run away, impressed him.

He became even more intrigued when she told him she was the daughter of Sammy Squirrel. He had heard of Sammy from several other creatures he knew, and now Snowy had told him they were moving to set up home in the forest, he decided he would keep a watch on them ...

*

It was now mid-Autumn, and the landscape was beginning to change. The fields looked barer and the hedges were losing their lush green foliage and turning a reddish brown. Trees were beginning to lose their leaves and a chilly wind swirled and whistled through the alleys and pathways. Many creatures were preparing for hibernation – a long, deep sleep which lasted through to the springtime – but Sammy and his family had never been busier, for they had many plans to make

16

and things to do before they could start their journey into the forest. Finally, after what seemed like endless delays and last-minute hitches, they were ready.

"Are we all set to go?" Sammy looked around at his family. They had already said their tearful farewells to the other squirrels who shared the dreys and nests. This included Mr. and Mrs. Dibbs and their children Rusty and Pippy, who hugged Slippy and Snowy for a long time before releasing them. Sammy didn't like farewells, and so, had hung back, only at the last moment shaking hands awkwardly with Mr. Dibbs, and giving Mrs. Dibbs a peck on the cheek.

"Come on," said Sammy. "This is it – let's get moving!"

On leaving the drey, the squirrels started to make their way across country. They ran across a deserted cricket pitch, over a narrow cycle track and footpath, and soon found themselves in a very large and beautiful green valley. The ground was covered with a thick carpet of golden leaves, and Snowy frivolously began to roll over and over in them, getting herself muddy and squealing in delight.

"Snowy Squirrel - that's quite enough of that!" cried Mrs. Squirrel. "You'll be a mess all day. Now, let's unpack some food and have a picnic."

Snowy poked her head out from a pile of leaves.

"Aren't you ever going to grow up?" said Slippy, shaking his head.

"Never!" Snowy replied, defiantly. She pulled a leaf from her tail and handed it to Slippy.

After a very tasty picnic of hazelnuts, acorns, conifer and walnut seeds, and delicious sweet chestnuts, they had a short rest before Sammy roused them once again.

"Come on, we can't stay here all day, we have to keep going."

So, they made their way through the valley, and journeyed on until the sun started to set. Soon it was too dark to see around them. "We'd better stop for the night," said Sammy. "We can make a drey in one of these trees, it doesn't have to be perfect, just good enough for one night."

And so, they all scurried around, collecting twigs, moss, and dry leaves, and soon they had a makeshift drey between the branches of a tall ash tree. Snowy was so tired she snuggled up to Slippy and was soon fast asleep. Slippy also could barely keep his eyes open, and soon all the squirrels were in the land of dreams, and up above, a clear half-moon and glittering stars watched over them.

The next morning, they started off again and made good progress until they came to the edge of a very wide lake.

"Oh my!" exclaimed Mrs. Squirrel. "What shall we do now?"

"Hmm," said Sammy, scratching his ears. "It's too wide to swim across, and I'm not fond of water. We will have to find another way to cross."

"I know where you can find a boat." The voice was bright and clear, and seemed to come out of nowhere. Sammy looked all around, but could see no other creature nearby, and then Snowy tugged at his arm and pointed to the lake.

Sammy took a step back, eyes wide with amazement, for emerging from the water was a young otter, who shook the water from his fur and joined them on the riverbank.

Sammy introduced himself and his family. "I'm called Ollie," said the otter. "There is an old boat that hasn't been used for years. Follow me, I'll show you where it is."

They bounded along after the otter, until they came to a broken-down jetty, and there, tied up in the water, was a small wooden rowing boat. It had obviously been left there for some time, and its paint was flaking off, but it was afloat, and looked strong enough to carry Sammy and his family across the lake. The otter unhooked the mooring rope and shouted. "Come on, jump in! I'll give you a push to get you started."

The squirrels clambered into the boat, and Sammy took the oars and began to row them across the river. The otter dived in and swam along beside them.

Things were going well until about half way across when Slippy noticed his feet were getting wet – the boat was starting to leak water!

"Oh no!" cried Mrs. Squirrel. "Slippy, quickly, find something to bail with." Slippy made a quick search of the boat, and under some dusty blankets, found an old rusty bucket.

"This will do," he stated, and began to bail the water out from the bottom of the boat. Sammy pulled hard on the oars, and soon they were close to the other bank of the river. Ollie called out to them, "You can do it, you're almost there!"

Slippy continued to bail for all he was worth, and Sammy strained on the oars. Snowy and Mrs. Squirrel held on to each other, shivering with apprehension.

A few minutes later they had reached the other side, and were sitting on the riverbank, trying to catch their breath. When they looked back, the boat started to fill with water, and rolling over on its side, sank down into the river.

"We only just made it," Sammy exclaimed.

"Well, only just is good enough!" Ollie replied. "I can lead you to the Rickety Bridge. Once you've crossed that, you are at the very edge of the forest."

"Thank you, Ollie," said Sammy, standing up.

"We must hurry, while there is still enough daylight – gather your things, and follow me."

*

Ollie led them towards the outskirts of the forest. It was growing colder and darker, but suddenly Ollie stopped and pointed up ahead. "There," he said. "There is the deep ravine, and the Rickety Bridge. You must cross it to get to the forest."

The ravine was a deep dark canyon, and Sammy could not see to the bottom. 'Even if you survived the fall, you would never be able to climb out again,' Sammy thought, as he surveyed the sheer steep walls of the rock-face. The Rickety Bridge looked fragile and dangerous as it swung to and fro in the rising wind. It was a very old footbridge. The ropes that held it in place looked worn, its wooden slats were in poor condition, and many sections had rotted away or were missing altogether.

"Is there any other way around?" Sammy turned to the otter.

"No," Ollie replied. "You cannot go by the river, it flows in the wrong direction. Besides, the bridge will hold, I've seen many animals cross it safely, but hurry, it's getting dark, and beginning to rain."

"Will you come with us?" Sammy asked the otter.

"I cannot." Ollie sounded sad. "My family will miss me, and I belong near the river, but I will wait until you are safely across." They shook hands, and then Sammy turned to Slippy and Snowy.

"We will go in pairs." I will go ahead with Mrs. Squirrel and the supplies. We must leave what we cannot carry. I will take the food across. Slippy, you will cross with Snowy – there's no time to waste!"

Sammy slung the sack of food over his shoulder and took Mrs. Squirrel by the hand.

"I'm scared, Sammy," she whispered.

"It will be fine – don't look down, just straight ahead."

Sammy tested the first slat of the bridge with his back foot, tapping it slightly. It felt strong enough. The rain was beginning to stop, and the wind had died down.

Sammy led Mrs. Squirrel over the Rickety Bridge. They were almost at the other side when there was a strong gust of wind, and the bridge swayed, knocking Sammy and Mrs. Squirrel off their feet, but they soon regained their balance and reached the last section of the bridge, which seemed stronger, and they were able to scamper across to the other side.

"There, that wasn't so bad," Sammy exclaimed. But Mrs. Squirrel looked very worried.

"Come on, little sister." Slippy tried his best to sound confident. "Just step where I step – stay close to me."

Carefully Slippy and Snowy began to cross over. Slippy stumbled on a loose slat, which dropped into the deep chasm below. He heard it shatter on the jagged rocks, and Slippy gulped, but said nothing. A steady rain began to fall again, and the wind grew stronger. The Rickety Bridge swung and creaked, and more slats fell behind them. The rain was making it difficult to get a proper foothold, and Slippy could not see ahead, as the wind was sweeping the rain into his face and eyes. Snowy whimpered, and Slippy turned to her and shouted. "Hang on to me, Snowy!"

Together they took each step, but it was taking a long time to get across. Finally, they reached the last section of the bridge, which felt a little safer, when suddenly the ropes holding the bridge behind them snapped – and the Rickety Bridge collapsed.

Slippy clung on to the remaining slats and clambered up. More slats fell, and the bridge twisted around, but Slippy held on and climbed up, reaching the edge of the ravine, where Sammy hauled him up towards safety.

But Snowy was in difficulty. She struggled to hang on to the wet ropes and slats and she started to slide down. Slippy caught Snowy's hand and began to pull her up towards him, but he couldn't get a firm enough grip, and Snowy was sliding away. "Climb, Snowy! Climb!" Slippy cried through the rain and wind.

Slippy couldn't hold Snowy any more. Her grip was weak and her little hand wasn't strong enough to pull herself up. Slippy stretched every sinew and tried desperately to hold on to her. The ropes holding the Rickety Bridge were straining and snapping. Lightning flashed in the sky.

And Snowy fell.

Slippy felt as though his heart had stopped.

Mrs. Squirrel closed her eyes.

Sammy stood perfectly still, a cold emptiness filling his mind.

A hideous silence.

On the far bank, Ollie gasped in horror.

Suddenly from out of nowhere a gigantic shadow descended, and a beat of wings could be heard above the wind. An enormous owl swooped down above their heads, and within seconds emerged again – holding a very small squirrel in its sharp lethal talons.

The owl placed Snowy down gently. Slippy covered his mouth. His whole body was shaking. Sammy put his arms around his shoulders, pulling him closer.

Snowy stirred, murmuring quietly. Mrs. Squirrel rushed to her and lifted her up, and then held on to her tightly, whispering, "My little Snowy, my little Snowy."

Snowy opened her eyes, and rubbed noses with Mrs. Squirrel. Sammy and Slippy embraced them both, and then Snowy saw Bramble, and scrambled over to him. She leapt up and clung on to him as if she would never let go. They all watched open-mouthed as Bramble wrapped Snowy in his huge wings, and began to rock her gently, cooing to her as if she were one of his own fledglings.

Chapter 3: Cousins

Silky spider hung above her web, waiting silently and patiently, her pincers ready for any creature unwise enough to get too close.

*

It was several days after the incident at the Rickety Bridge, and the squirrels had worked steadily to build a new drey. They had found the perfect place, in a wide Glade in the Great Forest, where many tall trees stood, and a small stream ran nearby. They had made their home between the forked branches of a very old oak tree, where they would be protected from the worst of the severe winter weather. They had also built several smaller dreys and nests nearby where they could rest between foraging excursions and store their food. Bramble had kindly brought their other goods over from across the ravine.

Slippy was very quiet, but the truth was, he had been badly shaken by the thought of losing Snowy, and in his nightmares, she was still falling.

Snowy, on the other hand, was becoming rebellious.

"I do not need protecting all the time!" she cried, and threw several acorns at Slippy, who had not left her side all morning.

"Mother told me to look after you!" Slippy stated.

"That doesn't mean you have to follow me around all day – I want to explore!"

Slippy sighed. "All right, I give in, but don't wander too far."

*

Sammy was busy constructing an overhead covering for the large drey they had built. The roof (he hoped) would keep the rain and snow from penetrating the drey, but it also needed to be strong enough to withstand the strong chill winds that whistled around the tree-tops.

It was now December, and the first snows had fallen. The days were shorter, and the nights longer and colder. Soon there would be little daylight time for foraging, and it would be too cold to stay out for long periods of time, so the squirrels would have to rely more and more on stored food to get them through the winter.

Sammy was very happy with the new drey. It had taken him a long time to construct, but it was very large, and contained several storage rooms for the abundant food they had collected. There was a wide variety of food in the forest. As well as the usual hazelnuts and acorns, Sammy, Mrs. Squirrel and Slippy had gathered many walnut seeds, pines and buds from the various trees around them, and best of all, Snowy had found a large supply of fruits and hornbeam which she gathered regularly and brought back from her large cache of food in the forest. She had also worked tirelessly on some underground burrows and nests where they could store emergency provisions if needed.

So, Sammy was content. He knew the winter would be harsh – they always were, but he was confident that they could survive until spring, when the days would lengthen, and foraging would be relatively easy.

In the meantime – he had to get back to work on the roof!

Slippy was angry with himself, and also worried about Snowy. She had been gone too long. What should he do? His first thought was to go out looking for her, but she could be anywhere in the Great Forest, and his chances of finding her were not very good. He paced around for a while, and then went to find Sammy, who was carefully examining a piece of timber, his ears twitching as he considered weights and measures ...

"Father, I'm sorry, but Snowy's wandered off again. I told her not to go far, but once she starts out somewhere there's no stopping her."

"I know," Sammy replied. "I was just the same at her age. The scrapes I used to get into!" Sammy shook his head. "I'm sure she will be all right, she's a little wild, but let her explore. It's the only way we learn – about ourselves, as well as others." Sammy stretched himself, and then continued to measure the piece of timber with his tail. "Oh yes," he added. "I forgot to mention – Bramble will be coming to stay with us soon. He has a few things to do first, but he should be here in the next few days. He will be making his roost in the large tree next to our drey."

Slippy was surprised and a little taken aback. "An owl – living with us? That's ... interesting. Father, do you think I should go and search for Snowy?"

Before Sammy could reply, Mrs. Squirrel approached, looking a little agitated.

"Sammy, I think you are needed. It looks like we have ... guests."

*

Snowy was enjoying the sense of freedom she had felt when they had finally arrived in the forest. There was so much space, and so many great places to see. She loved being in the forest, she loved the trees and the small ponds, the bracken and the old trails that led to nowhere in particular. She waited a while until Slippy was called in to do his chores, and then climbed much higher, and started to leap from tree to tree effortlessly. She was on her way to explore!

She had covered quite a distance and found some wonderful hiding places to store all kinds of food. She was busy digging up some roots when she heard a furious rustling noise, and some whimpering sounds of distress. She immediately became alert, and raced up the nearest tree. It sounded like another squirrel was nearby, and for a moment, she thought that Slippy had followed her deep into the woods. But, somehow, she knew it wasn't Slippy. She carefully made her way back down the tree and quietly edged towards the rustling sound. And then she saw – it was another squirrel, but not Slippy, and he was groaning in anguish. She moved closer, and could see it was a young, grey squirrel, and he was trapped.

The grey squirrel looked up at her helplessly. "I've got my foot caught in this tree hollow. It's all tangled up in the roots and foliage."

"Let me help you," said Snowy, and began to untwist the vines and roots of the fallen tree, using her sharp teeth to cut through the foliage.

The two young squirrels eyed each other uncertainly.

"Your fur," he said, "it's completely red."

"Well, I suppose it is," Snowy replied. "I've never really thought about it."

"And your tail – your tail is ... different."

"And your fur is grey, and so thick, and your tail is nearly all white."

"Our tails turn white in the winter, but then turn back to grey in the spring."

"That's a neat trick, but my tail is always like this."

"And you are so small, are you a kit?"

"No, I am not a kit!" Snowy replied sharply. "I am nearly two! And my brother is even older! Though only by a few minutes," she added quietly.

"You have family here?"

"Yes, we've only just moved into the forest. It's amazing here, isn't it?"

"Well, I suppose," said the grey squirrel. "I've lived here all my life – I'm nearly three!"

"What's your name?" Snowy asked.

"I'm called Joey."

Suddenly a twig snapped behind them and Snowy turned around, and saw a sleek and menacing creature emerge from the shadows.

Snowy instinctively drew back. She had never seen this hunter before, but she had heard the most awful stories – for she had recognized the creature at once.

It was a pine-marten.

And it was moving closer.

*

Silky Spider felt a tug on her web. She spun some more silk and moved in for a closer view. She couldn't be sure, but it looked hopeful. And then her pincers began to wave around in the air. Something was caught in her trap ...

*

The pine-marten was a lithe, weasel-like creature, with brown and cream coloured fur, large ears, and dark, penetrating eyes.

"Hate to interrupt your little conversation." The pine-marten's voice was raspy, and he spoke with an arrogance that Snowy didn't like at all. He looked first at Joey. "Your sort I know very well," he smiled maliciously, and then he looked at Snowy with disdain. "And you, you are so tiny you are hardly worth my trouble. But as you are both trespassing in my territory ..." And he lunged straight towards Joey, whose foot was still half-stuck in the foliage of the tree roots.

Snowy didn't hesitate, but leapt between them, which confused the pine-marten enough for him to momentarily lose his balance.

"Try me first!" Snowy exclaimed.

The pine-marten turned angrily on Snowy.

"You play dangerous games, tiny squirrel. Now – run!" And he rushed at Snowy with gaping jaws.

But Snowy didn't run. She side-stepped in a split second so the pine-marten's jaws snapped on thin air. This made him even angrier. "Now I will teach you what fear is," he snarled viciously.

"I'll never run from you." Snowy replied, and she jumped up onto the lowest branch of the nearest tree.

The pine-marten was swift, and very clever, but every time he got close to Snowy she somehow evaded him, making him climb higher. They skipped and jumped rapidly from tree to tree, but Snowy was always just one leap ahead. Each time the pine-marten thought that he had caught her she doubled back, and leapt towards him, confusing him, and making him turn sharply. Snowy was climbing higher and higher. The pine-marten was struggling to keep up with her, she was so swift and agile, and she moved so gracefully, and seemingly without effort. She was making the pine-marten look slow and heavy, even though he was an excellent climber.

Snowy could easily have escaped him then, across the canopy of the highest trees, but instead of this she continued to double back, so they were constantly leaping around in circles.

Snowy could sense that the pine-marten was growing tired. She increased her pace a little, and was soon at the top of the very highest trees. The pine-marten was getting anxious and frustrated. For all his speed and cleverness, he was being out-manoeuvred, and he felt that she was toying with him. And then he made an error of judgment, and leapt onto a branch that could not hold his weight. He slipped and fell onto a lower branch, and then tumbled to the ground, twisting his body in mid-air, so he landed heavily but safely on his feet.

Snowy raced down from the tree-tops and sat in exactly the same place where she had started from. Joey had freed his foot from the roots and was gazing at her, round-eyed. The pine-marten was puffing and panting. His body was bruised and he had the wind knocked out of him. Snowy had hardly drawn breath.

"I told you I'd never run from you," said Snowy. "I might run around you, but never from you."

"Well," the pine-marten hissed through his teeth. "You have out-witted me, little squirrel. Go now, both of you – and do not return this way again. You may not be so lucky next time!"

The pine-marten backed away and disappeared into the forest. In truth he was sorely wounded and shaken from his fall, and would need several days to recover.

Snowy turned back to Joey.

"Can you walk?"

"I can try," Joey stammered. "You were just wonderful, Snowy."

"He made me angry," Snowy replied. "He tried to frighten me and bully me, and I've never liked bullies. I had to show him he couldn't push me around."

"I was so scared. I'm not brave like you, Snowy."

"But I was scared, Joey," Snowy responded. "I just couldn't let him attack you like that – it wasn't fair – and anyone would think that he owned the forest the way he spoke, but nobody can own the forest. The forest is here for all of us. Anyway, are you sure you can walk?"

"It's a bit painful, but yes, I think it will be okay."

"Well, come back with me and we will fix you up properly. You can meet my family."

*

Silky Spider hurried to the centre of her web, but she was too late. The fly had dislodged itself, and escaped.

*

Snowy and Joey made their way back through the forest. By the time they approached the Glade, Joey needed to lean on Snowy to help him along. They hesitated as they drew closer to the dreys.

Something was happening. Snowy could see her parents and Slippy standing together in the middle of the Glade, and surrounding them were a large group of grey squirrels. The largest of the greys was approaching Sammy. He was obviously their leader. Sammy stood still, saying nothing, but meeting the large grey's piercing stare. There was a feeling of uncertainty and uneasiness, then suddenly Joey called out.

"Father, I'm back. I got lost in the forest. This is Snowy. She's my friend. She saved me from a hideous pine-marten."

The leader of the grey squirrels turned to Joey with much relief.

"Oh, there you are son, your mother and I were getting worried about you."

Several of the female grey squirrels scurried over to Joey and carried him to the centre of the Glade, where they laid him down and started to examine his foot.

Snowy was suddenly tired, but leapt over to her parents who hugged her tightly.

Mrs. Squirrel spoke to the grey squirrels leaning over Joey.

"You'll need some herbs," she said. "We have plenty here. Let us help you."

The atmosphere suddenly relaxed, and Sammy and the leader of the grey squirrels shook hands and embraced each-other.

"What's this about a pine-marten?" Sammy asked Snowy, looking concerned.

"Oh, it was nothing, father." Snowy yawned. "Just a silly game."

"It wasn't nothing!" Joey exclaimed, and looked around at all the grey squirrels. "She didn't run away, she out-tricked him – she was incredible." And with that he immediately fell asleep.

All eyes were on Snowy, but she was also in the land of dreams, and Mrs. Squirrel covered her with a blanket and carried her inside.

"She'll sleep for hours," she said quietly.

"I'll watch over her," said Slippy. "My brave little sister."

Sammy turned to their guests.

"You are welcome to stay with us tonight. We have plenty of good food stored up, some excellent fruit, and some red-berry wine!"

The leader of the grey squirrels beamed at Sammy.

"Thank you, Sammy, we would be delighted to join you." He looked around at the other greys. "Well, don't just stand there – come along and meet your cousins!"

Chapter 4: The Waterfall

Sammy scrutinized the pieces of wood in front of him, and then studied the meticulous plans he had sketched. All morning he'd been working on the roof covering for the drey, but for some reason the measurements did not add up, and he was struggling to work out how to construct it.

The morning was very bright, the birds were singing, and the sun shone through the trees in the Glade. Sammy muttered to himself, and then flung down his tools in frustration, and began to pace up and down, wondering what to try next.

Their guests had stayed late, and Sammy had exchanged many stories and tall tales with the leader of their grey cousins, whose name was Squirrel Stanley. Now, Squirrel Stanley was also an excellent story-teller, and he and Sammy had begun a strong friendship, laughing long into the night at each other's colourful adventures.

Perhaps Sammy had partaken of a little too much berry-wine, for he had a slight headache, which was getting worse as he tried to make sense of the measurements for the new roof structure.

Sammy looked up at the sky. It was going to be a fine day. The December winds had dropped, and it did not feel as cold as it had been.

Mrs. Squirrel had left earlier. She was a wonderful healer, and she was visiting their new cousins to make sure that Joey's foot was mending as it should. So that left Slippy and Snowy. Sammy's ears began to twitch. Perhaps a break from work today would do them all good, and Sammy knew the perfect place to take the two of them.

"Yes, that's it!" he exclaimed, and called out to his children, who were both preparing to go out foraging again.

"Never mind that now," said Sammy. "We're going on an excursion. I want to show you something – deep in the heart of the Great Forest." And Sammy leapt up the nearest tree. "Come on, you two slouches, see if you can keep up with the old man!"

*

Mrs. Squirrel had finished cleaning Joey's foot and was applying some herbs to the wound when his mother, Mrs. Rose, entered the bed-chamber. "Will he be all right?" she asked anxiously.

"Oh yes. Give him plenty to eat and fresh water, and let him rest for a few days. You must also clean the wound and apply these herbs twice a day."

"Thank you – he told me all about Snowy, and how brave she was."

"Yes, but I worry about her sometimes – she should be more careful."

"We all worry, Mrs. Squirrel. As soon as you have kits, it's a normal state of affairs."

"I know – but Snowy!" Mrs. Squirrel lifted her hands in resignation.

"She's just young and boisterous – but she has such a large heart."

Mrs. Squirrel looked away, and could say nothing.

"And Sammy!" Mrs. Rose continued. "It must be ... interesting being married to such a character!"

"Interesting is one way of putting it!" Mrs. Squirrel shook her head. "Oh my, I really must have been mad!"

"I cannot possibly comment, being married to Squirrel Stanley! Oh dear, I think we were both mad," cried Mrs. Rose.

They looked at each other and began to laugh, until the tears streamed down their faces.

*

Sammy led Slippy and Snowy deep into the woods, leaping from tree to tree and branch to branch. Slippy was amazed at how quickly Sammy could still move, and Snowy was calling out in delight as she followed. She let Sammy lead the way, watching his every trick, and marvelling at his agility. She felt completely at home in the trees, and some days she never touched the ground, but would stay aloft and climb and jump until she was too tired to leap any more, and then she would find an old hollow or used drey, and sleep until the sunrise woke her.

Slippy was a little slower, and tended to lag behind, staying aware of all that was around him. But still he was capable of strong bursts of speed, and his strength meant that he had no fear of anything once he was aloft.

Sammy began to slow down, and let the others catch up with him.

"Well, that was fun!" He stated. "We're almost there let's get to the ground, we should go on foot the rest of the way."

And so, they climbed down to the forest floor, which was completely covered in dry leaves, twigs, and plant-life.

As they moved on through the woodlands Snowy was the first to hear it – the mighty roar of falling water, and when they crossed a large clearing and came out the other side they saw it – a formidable, dangerous, and staggeringly beautiful waterfall.

*

Snowy and Slippy gasped, and Sammy stared at the spectacular sight.

"Isn't it amazing?" Sammy mused, in a voice that sounded far away.

"It's wonderful!" cried Snowy, jumping up and down in excitement.

"It's incredible, just incredible." Slippy sounded completely awestruck.

"This is the very heart of the woodlands," Sammy explained. "From here, everything grows."

"But where does so much water come from?" asked Slippy.

"The rivers, the lakes – all flowing towards the great ocean – it is the continuing cycle of nature."

"Father!" cried Snowy. "Look – I can see something moving in the water!"

"It is the salmon," Sammy answered. "Every year they return to spawn and create new life, in the very rivers they were birthed in."

For a time, none of them spoke, and then Snowy heard a splashing sound nearby, and found a series of shallow rock pools. In one of these pools, a large fish was struggling.

"Oh," Sammy was shocked. "It is a salmon, caught in a rock pool. We must try to return him to the river." Snowy leaned over the rock pool, full of curiosity.

"How did you get in here?" she asked the salmon.

"I misjudged my leap, and landed on the bank – I managed to wriggle to this pool, but I must get back to the river – can you help me?"

"Of course," Sammy replied. "We'd be glad to."

"This is my final journey," the salmon explained. "I return with the others, to produce our young, and then, I shall die."

"Then we will be helping to kill you!" cried Snowy, in exasperation.

"No, no, little squirrel – you will be saving me – so I can complete the journey that has always been my destiny. And if you do not help me, I shall surely die in this pool of mud, alone, and with no offspring."

Snowy turned towards her father with tears in her eyes, but Sammy lowered himself over the pool.

"Now, Slippy, help me – take off your jacket – we must carry him between us – careful now. He will be heavy."

Sammy also pulled off his jacket, and then tied the two jackets together to make a kind of hammock to hold the salmon.

They lowered the makeshift hammock over the edge of the pool and the salmon wriggled on top of it. Between the two of them, and with much trouble, Sammy and Slippy managed to partly carry and partly drag the salmon from the pool and across to the river bank. The salmon was soon struggling to breathe, but fortunately it was only a very short distance to the river's edge.

"Thank you, and may you thrive." The salmon gasped, as they lowered him down into the water. They watched him until he was just another speck in the great river, on his final journey, swimming against the tide.

Snowy was clearly distressed, and made little sobbing noises, but Sammy beckoned her towards a rock, where they all sat down and watched the waterfall.

Sammy spoke to his children:

"Don't be sad for the salmon – he has seen wonders in the great ocean that we can only dream of – and had many an exciting adventure, no doubt! He has fulfilled his purpose, and now returns to the very place of his birth, to give thanks for his life, and help to create new life. In the spring, the young will hatch, and so the great cycle of life repeats, changing and yet unchanged, for all eternity and beyond. It is nature's way of replenishing herself, of giving back to the lands, the seas, the skies. Every creature in our world is part of this great cycle of life – it is a noble thing, is it not?"

Snowy had grown very quiet, and Slippy was thoughtful. They sat for a long time, watching the huge waterfall, and the salmon – thousands of them, making their journeys upstream.

"And when our time comes, father?" Slippy asked quietly.

Sammy grinned down at them both.

"Time comes for all of us, Slippy – every creature can only live out the lifetime they are given, it is the way of all things – and you have so many special years ahead!"

Slippy opened his mouth to speak, but could find no words, and Snowy looked up at her father with great affection, holding his hand, and then she looked back at the waterfall, still overwhelmed by its power and beauty.

*

Mrs. Squirrel had made a wonderful new friend in Mrs. Rose. They hugged one another before Mrs. Squirrel left to return to the Glade where she had set up her new home with Sammy. She never hurried, but moved gracefully from tree to tree, until she reached the Glade, and there, much to her surprise, was a most welcome guest.

"Bramble!" I'm so happy to see you!" she cried.

Bramble spread his wings and chuckled. "I was wondering if I'd come to the right place," he said, "there was nobody around. I was about to fly off and search for you."

"Oh, don't worry," Mrs. Squirrel replied. "Sammy and the children have gone off somewhere – Sammy has left me a message."

Mrs. Squirrel picked up a leaf, shaped like a heart, which Sammy had left under a stone on one of the pieces of timber he was working on.

"This has always been a message that all is well, and that he will return soon. I think I know where they have gone. Now, you must be tired – have you flown a long way? You must tell me all the news. Come inside and let me show you around our new home – there's plenty of good places for you to roost."

*

The three squirrels took their time returning to the Glade. On the way back they made several detours, and Snowy showed Sammy and Slippy where she had cached a large quantity of food for winter. Sammy couldn't help but be impressed with her ability to always find the best places, and her hard work at maintaining the food supplies.

They drew nearer to home, and as the skies darkened overhead, Sammy turned to his children.

"Ah, I do believe that your mother is back from her visit."

"Oh, I do hope that Joey is all right," said Snowy.

"I'm sure he will be – Mrs. Squirrel will take good care of him."

"Mother has been teaching me how to heal," Snowy replied, "but I'm finding it quite difficult. There's so much to learn – plants and herbs, leaves and flowers, all kind of things."

"Just take your time, healing is a true art, and cannot be learned or taught overnight. It took your mother years to become a true healer."

"How's the roof coming on, father?" asked Slippy, quietly, as he knew full well that it wasn't going according to plan.

"I just don't understand why I can't make sense of it all!" Sammy cried. "I've gone over and over it – I've tried everything, but nothing works!" He threw his hands up in frustration.

Snowy gave the plans a cursory glance and then looked briefly at the rows of timber.

"That's because it's upside-down, father. You've got it the wrong way round." She yawned. "I'm very tired now. I'll see you both tomorrow." And with that she scampered up a tree, into one of the smaller dreys, and immediately fell asleep.

Sammy and Slippy looked at each-other, bewildered, and then at the drey where Snowy was sleeping, then at the plans, and then at the timber. Sammy rubbed his chin, and his ears started to twitch.

"Well I go to sea!" he exclaimed. "Why didn't I think of that?"

Slippy shuffled his feet, and said nothing.

Sammy pointed at Slippy.

"Not a word of this to your mother – I mean not one word!"

Sammy looked serious.

Slippy nodded dumbly.

*

They entered the large drey, and were overjoyed to find Bramble had joined them.

"How was your excursion?" asked Mrs. Squirrel.

"Oh, it was amazing, mum," Slippy replied. "We saw the waterfall, the salmon, everything. Snowy is sleeping. She's worn out."

"Oh, the waterfall – isn't it wonderful!"

"You've seen it, mum?"

"Yes indeed, your father took me there the first week we arrived when you and Snowy were out foraging."

Sammy beamed at Mrs. Squirrel, who suddenly looked embarrassed.

"Well, let's have some tea," she said, fumbling with the cutlery.

Soon they were all eating and drinking, and Bramble told them he had already found the perfect tree to roost in.

"If I could take a few small pieces of timber, it would be even better, Sammy."

"Of course," said Sammy. "Now I've figured out how to do the roof cover, there will be plenty of wood left over." And he winked at Slippy mischievously.

Chapter 5: Felix

Felix was having the same dream again. He squirmed and twisted in his sleep, unable to stop the haunting images in his mind.

The hounds were gaining with every heartbeat. The horses' hooves growing louder and louder, and the terrifying blast of the hunting horn sounding ominously close. The foxes scrambled through thickets and hedges, running for their lives, but they could not get clear of the hounds, who raced after them with huge leaps, hungry for their scent.

The foxes reached a large open field, where there was no cover. Two of the foxes exchanged glances with the others – two adults carrying cubs – they nodded, and then ran across the field, the hounds yelping and tearing after them. The foxes holding the cubs looked lost and bewildered, not knowing which way to run. They were desperately turning around in blind panic, when suddenly a young squirrel appeared out of nowhere.

"Quickly – follow me!"

Without hesitation the foxes followed the squirrel, who led them down a narrow pathway, across a small bridge, and into a wooded area. Here they saw a small shallow stream, running down away from the town.

"Hurry!" cried the squirrel. "You must follow the stream until the hounds lose your scent." The squirrel leapt up a tree and over to the other side of the stream. The foxes lifted their cubs onto their backs and waded into the water. They moved as fast as they could, but it was slow going through the stream. The young squirrel moved on ahead, and after what seemed like an age, he stopped by some dense foliage.

"Over here, that's right, now dig down a bit, and you'll find a small fox-hole – stay in there – I'll see if I can help the others."

Exhausted and shaking, the foxes dug where the squirrel had shown them, and sure enough, there was an old fox den, just large enough for them to hide in. Here they waited and recovered, gasping for breath. They could hear the hounds baying in the distance, but after a time the sounds grew fainter, and eventually there was only the pounding of their own hearts. They waited until curiosity got the better of them, and they were just about to emerge from the den, when the squirrel appeared and joined them inside.

"I'm sorry." The young squirrel looked crestfallen. "I couldn't save the other two foxes – the hounds caught them in the open field – it was dreadful."

"Oh no, no!" cried the vixen. "Poor Bobby and Fern! What about their cubs, Tricksy and sweet little Skip?" and she burst into tears.

"I know where they are hidden," the dog fox replied quietly. "Once the hunt has moved away, I'll go and fetch them. We will raise them as our own – we must be their parents now." He lowered his head. "Bobby and Fern gave their lives for us. They drew the hounds away so we would have a chance to escape."

The dog fox approached the squirrel.

"I don't know how to thank you," he spoke softly. "If you hadn't helped us, we too would have been caught by the hounds."

"I'm only sorry I couldn't help the others," said the squirrel, with sadness in his voice. "But I couldn't get to them quickly enough."

"You tried, at least," the fox replied. "What are you called?"

"I'm Sammy," the young squirrel replied. "You are safe now, at least for a while."

"Thanks to you, my friend."

"Why will they never leave us alone?" cried the vixen. "We haven't been near their farm for years, yet still they set the hounds on us. Why can we never be free?"

"I don't know." Sammy shook his head. "But you will never be safe this close to the humans – you must move away from here to raise and protect your cubs."

An instant later the younger of the two cubs ran out of the den, but before his parents could go after him he returned, holding a flower in his jaws. He approached Sammy timidly and placed the flower at Sammy's feet. It was a small wild daffodil. The little cub lay down and looked at Sammy with round serious eyes.

Sammy picked up the flower and held it close to him.

"Thank you, son," he whispered.

The fox cub was too young to speak yet, but gave a sharp little bark to Sammy.

"Well done, Felix, well done." The dog fox beamed at his son with pride.

Felix awoke and looked around him. Again, the dream had come, leaving him restless and shaken. He felt something pulling at him, urging him to be somewhere else. It wasn't quite dawn yet, but he already knew it would be a fine bright day. The heaviness of the dream slowly left him, and he sat down quietly and began to think.

After encountering Sammy's children and recovering the collar they had lost, he had thought about the past, and how his parents had raised four cubs, two of their own, himself and his sister Fis, and also Tricksy and Skip, whom Felix had a great love for.

Felix had grown tired of living near the town. The roads were too dangerous, there was less food and less woodland than there had been when he was a cub.

He had heard that Sammy and his family had moved to the Great Forest, and he felt it would be a good idea to join them there, and perhaps help Sammy at the same time if he could. In any case, it would be good to see the old rascal again, and hear of his adventures.

Felix stretched and yawned as the sun began to climb higher over the hills. He knew that winter weather was on its way, but for now, he should make the most of the bright day. He sat up and scratched his ears, then he began to clean his fur, taking his time before he moved off.

He wandered down to a small pond for his morning drink. There were several ducks and swans swimming along the glassy surface of the water, but many were staying indoors, preparing for winter, and keeping warm.

Felix was just about to take his drink when he was interrupted by a familiar croaky voice.

"Good morning, Mr. Fox!" Felix looked up, into the eyes of a very fat, very ugly, toad, who was sitting on a water-lily in the middle of the pond.

"Good morning to you, Mr. Quirk – I trust you are well this morning?"

"Oh yes, can't complain, Mr. Fox, but if you don't mind me saying, you look a little tired."

"Yes, I am," said Felix. "I didn't sleep very well – I have the same recurring dreams."

"Ah," said Mr. Quirk. "I think perhaps something plays on your mind, Mr. Fox?"

"Well," Felix replied. "I have been thinking about making a journey – to go and live in the Great Forest. There is very little left for me here."

"Yes indeed," Mr. Quirk sounded a little despondent. "The ponds grow fewer, the woodlands disappear, and the winters seem to linger on – but maybe that's just my advanced years talking."

"No, I think you are right, Mr. Quirk. I have been feeling unsettled for some time. Perhaps it is time for me to move on."

"I will miss your company, Mr. Fox, but I don't blame you for wishing to leave. I will stay here and see out the end of my days, but you are still young – you will wish to raise your own cubs soon. I think you would do better in the forest."

"Yes, I must leave," Felix replied. "I will miss our little chats, Mr. Quirk, and your sound advice."

"Ah, thank you, Mr. Fox. If only I took my own advice more often!" They both chuckled at this, and then Mr. Quirk grew serious.

"It is no easy journey to the Great Forest. You must cross the river, and the deep ravine."

"I will find a way," said Felix. "There is always a way, if you look hard enough."

"I'm sure you will, Mr. Fox. "I wish you the very best of luck – and if you see Sammy Squirrel, tell him from me that he is a rogue – I haven't forgotten our last adventure together!"

"I'll tell him you said so," Felix replied, with a laugh. "Well, good luck to you, and farewell."

"Farewell, Mr. Fox," said the toad, and he hopped off the water-lily and disappeared into the bull-rushes.

Felix was a little saddened after saying goodbye to Mr. Quirk, whom he had known for many years, but he was fully resolved now to begin his journey. Yes, he would leave the grimy town, the grimy houses, and the busy roads – he would join Sammy and his friends in the forest!

And Felix moved off swiftly, with a renewed purpose in his steps.

Chapter 6: Spirits

In the depths of the forest, something stirred.

There was a general stillness, as though the Great Forest was holding its breath, and then the stirring began again, and from the thickest undergrowth, Shade emerged. Her cold black eyes penetrated the early morning mist, and she could feel the fresh wind and drizzle of rain in the air.

Shade slithered her way to a deep pool of water for her morning swim. She loved the feel of the cool water cleansing her scales and clearing her mind.

Once back on dry land she shook off the last of her drowsiness, and felt a pang of hunger.

Shade's senses became sharp, and her long tongue flickered. There were no other creatures nearby, but this did not surprise her. It was almost time for her to hibernate through the cold, bleak winter – just one more hunt should be enough. As she moved slowly and deliberately through the undergrowth, birds scattered above her, and she heard the hurried scampering of many smaller animals fleeing deeper into the woods.

Shade was not concerned, she was very patient. Snakes never hurry, and Shade was a fully grown, fully alert adder, and it was time for her to feed.

*

In another part of the forest something very unusual was happening. A long funnel of bats suddenly came pouring forth from the mouth of a deep cave hidden in the rocks. Their fluttering, jerky, twisty flight spoke of confusion and fear. Their hibernation had been interrupted, and they were completely disorientated. For several minutes they flew around aimlessly, until at last they perched down to rest in the branches of some tall trees.

Bramble was returning to his home in the Glade when he noticed this, and he glided down swiftly to ask them what the matter was.

*

Sammy yawned, and stretched, and yawned again. He stood back, satisfied with his handiwork. With Bramble's help he had managed to complete the roof covering for the drey, and it was none too soon, for the coming winter threatened to be a harsh one, and he could sense that heavy snow would be falling soon.

He had been unable to sleep, as ever since dusk the roaring and bellowing of stags could be heard in the distance, as they clashed antlers for the right of leadership over the herds. The strongest would prevail, the weaker would be forced to submit and wait another year for another chance. The sounds of their struggles echoed through the forest, and every creature stopped in their tracks, spellbound by the sounds of the fighting, until finally, it was settled. There was a long moment of silence, and then the triumphant stag announced his victory with a huge blood-curdling bellow, and all creatures of the forest lowered their heads to acknowledge the new lord of the woodlands.

The struggle had lasted for most of the night, and Sammy had given up trying to sleep, risen early, and decided to complete the work on the roof covering.

As Sammy yawned once more he heard the familiar fluttering of wings, and Bramble flew down onto a nearby branch. He seemed to have been hurrying, and he was ruffled and short of breath.

Bramble took a moment to compose himself.

"Sammy, I must speak with you – something strange has occurred – the bats … they are terrified. Something in the cave …"

"Slow down," said Sammy. "Come in out of this drizzle and tell me all about it."

*

It had taken Felix two days to reach the river that Sammy and his family had crossed on their way to the forest. Felix was no great swimmer, so he sat on the riverbank, looked up at the clouds, and pondered.

"Hmm, it will rain soon, and I cannot cross here," he thought. "But there must be another way."

Felix was a very patient fox, and he began to pad along the edge of the riverbank.

Further along, Felix noticed a long thin boat by the riverside. It was a barge, and it was being poled along by two men around a curve where the river narrowed. Felix had no idea where it was going, but there was now a drizzly rain coming down, and Felix felt the need for shelter. The men were distracted, concentrating on steering the barge, so Felix ghosted his way closer, and slipped onto the boat and hid under some tarpaulin, awaiting his chance to reach the opposite side of the river.

*

"We must investigate," Sammy exclaimed. "This could be important for all of us." Sammy had gathered his family around him and told them Bramble's story. "It is very odd that bats should be driven out of a deep cave like this. We have to move quickly, and follow Bramble. The rain is easing a little, so we need to leave immediately. Snowy – Slippy, bring some food, we can eat something on the way."

And so, the squirrels set off, with Bramble leading them, flying low above them. They made rapid progress, and after a bite to eat, were soon approaching the location of the hidden cave. The squirrels climbed over some craggy rocks and boulders that surrounded the entrance to the cave.

"Here, this is the place," said Bramble. "I will come in with you, but tread very carefully – it will be too dark to see anything properly."

The closer they got to the mouth of the cave, the more Sammy felt a sense of uneasiness. No birds – crows, ravens or magpies, could be seen or heard, and the sunlight, which had been quite bright during their journey, was gone, leaving only a shadowy darkness all around them. It was not a cold day for the time of year, but even Snowy was shivering.

"I don't like this, Sammy – something isn't right here," Mrs. Squirrel sounded frightened.

"No," said Sammy, sniffing the air. "The scent is all wrong."

"Look, father," Snowy whispered, "footprints, leading right up to the cave."

Sammy's ears twitched. "I don't recognise these footprints," he stated. "They are not of our kind, and they are too large for most creatures."

"They look more like a large dog's paw prints," Snowy replied, examining them closely. "But they are old prints, very old, worn deep into the ground."

A wind began to bluster, and there was a sudden clap of thunder. Heavy rain started to beat down upon the surrounding rocks.

"Come on!" cried Sammy, "let's get inside the cave – at least it will be dry."

*

Felix had been very lucky. The barge he had boarded had soon reached a narrow stretch of the winding river, and he had managed to leap onto the opposite riverbank, unseen by the men, who never once suspected that they had carried a stowaway on board.

The rain grew steadier, but now there was the cover of trees and woodlands, and Felix breathed a sigh of relief, and hurried on towards the ravine.

*

The squirrels looked around them nervously. The cave's walls were damp and cold, and it was treacherous underfoot, with many loose stones and rocks scattered across the floor of the cave.

"Stay close, and tread carefully," Sammy warned the others. "Bramble, can you see anything?"

"Not a thing, Sammy," Bramble replied.

Another rumble of thunder echoed around the cave.

"Very well, let's just stay here for a while, and have a think." Sammy was unsure what to do next, and he felt edgy. He fully agreed with Mrs. Squirrel – something didn't feel right about this place.

Some time passed, and the storm outside abated, but the drizzly rain persisted, and inside the cave, the squirrels were colder than ever.

Sammy and the others had carefully begun to explore the interior of the cave as their eyes grew accustomed to the darkness. As they searched, it became clear that the floor of the cave was littered not only with stones and rocks, but also with the bones of long-dead animals.

"These bones are too large for most creatures," Sammy whispered to Bramble. "What do you make of them?"

"Snowy was right," Bramble replied. "The footprints outside seem to be paw-prints, and these bones are large enough to belong to a dog, or a larger creature – but what would they be doing here?"

"Perhaps there was an inner chamber?" Sammy ventured. "And maybe ..." Sammy became animated. "Maybe something was buried or lost here?"

"Very good!" Suddenly a harsh, commanding voice echoed around the cavern, and a luminous glow lit up the interior of the cave, where flickering shadows danced upon the walls.

The squirrels huddled together, with Bramble standing behind them. They turned around in horror and disbelief, for all around them, surrounding them in the strange ghost-light, was a huge pack of savage-looking wolves.

Sammy hardly dared to breathe, as one of the wolves, no doubt the pack leader, paced slowly towards them.

Even through his fear Sammy realised this was a she-wolf, unusual for a pack-leader, but she had the grace and confidence of command. A strange aura surrounded her, and her cold grey eyes burned deep into Sammy's. For a long time she said nothing, and Sammy held her gaze.

"You have courage," she spoke quietly, but her voice still filled the cave. "Know then that I am Siana, and all that you see in this cave is no more."

Suddenly the walls of the cave were brighter, luminous, and Sammy could make out the ancient shapes and images of many beasts – bears, bison, a ferocious-looking wild-cat with sabre-like teeth, a huge woolly creature with enormous tusks, and several other creatures he didn't recognise.

"All that you see has been hunted down and destroyed. We are the spirits of many creatures who once lived in these woods. The wolves were the last to perish. We were being hunted down by men with dogs. We ran in here – one of our sacred places, so we could die with our forebears, but we were too late – we couldn't get deep enough into the cave. The dogs found us and there was a long and brutal fight. We held the dogs off, but when the men arrived with guns we were all slain. And now our spirits are trapped between worlds, unable to move on, unable to rest.

"The gunfire caused part of the cavern to collapse, and our bones – our remains, lay near the entrance to the cave. They have lain there for hundreds of years, outside our sacred place of rest, and our souls have nowhere to go, but wander ceaselessly in the void, the great void of nothingness ..."

The wolves began to howl, and Sammy's heart was full of grief, but suddenly Snowy stepped forward, and all fear seemed to have left her.

"Father," she said, softly. "I know why we are here – there is a well, in the inner chamber. We must dig through the collapsed wall and place their bones around the well so their spirits can join their predecessors. It is the only way for them to find peace."

Siana moved towards Snowy and studied her closely.

"You are wise, little squirrel, we have waited long for you." She looked deep into Snowy's eyes. "Yes, this one has the gift – she knows what to do."

"Yes, I know." Snowy replied, looking up at Siana, unflinchingly. "We will help you."

*

Felix looked down into the depths of the ravine. Most creatures would have been disheartened by such a formidable sight, but Felix had already crossed the river, and so he felt undaunted by the sheer drop and width of the enormous chasm. He would stay patient, and keep moving.

Felix padded along the edge of the ravine for some time. He knew a storm was brewing, and, sure enough, a rumble of thunder could be heard overhead. The rain grew heavier, and the wind became bitterly cold. He was getting soaked through, and knew he must stop and find some proper shelter soon.

Just as the rain and wind were making him feel weary and despondent, a flash of lightning tore through the sky and struck one of the larger trees on the other side of the canyon. Felix looked up through the driving rain, and gasped as the huge tree groaned and toppled, its roots unearthed. There was a tremendous tearing and wrenching sound, and the tree fell, smashing through heather, foliage and bracken – right across the ravine!

He waited for several minutes, until he was certain the great tree had come to rest. The long branches were stretched out over the canyon, and Felix knew this was his chance to get across. He approached the fallen tree warily, and felt the strength of the larger boughs – they should easily hold his weight – and the trunk itself was still very strong, despite the damage from the lightning.

And so, Felix carefully edged his way along the fallen branches and the mighty trunk of the great tree. It took some time, and he had to take special care not to slip, but after several hair-raising minutes, he reached the other side of the ravine.

Felix was very tired by now. He found some thick foliage and dug down, trying desperately to construct a makeshift 'earth' to keep himself out of the storm. His weary limbs responded slowly, but he managed to dig out a small area, at least enough to stay dry for now, and he snuck down to rest and recover his strength.

The worst part of his journey was over, and once the storm had passed, all he had to do was find Sammy and his family – four small squirrels in a very large forest!

*

It had taken the whole day for the squirrels and Bramble to carefully dig their way through the collapsed wall of rock and stones. It was dangerous work, but eventually they were able to make a passage-way into the inner chamber of the cave, and place the wolves' remains around the well in the centre.

As they watched, something amazing happened. The shattered bones seemed to merge together, forming the luminous shape of a large wolf, and then, miraculously, the bones sunk into the ground, and vanished completely.

The sound of running water could be heard from below.

"An underground stream," Sammy whispered.

The spirits of the wolves appeared, and Siana came forward.

"Yes," Siana's voice came from all around them. "It is part of the stream of life that runs between the worlds. Now we can be at peace at last. Thank you, Sammy Squirrel, for bringing her to us." And once more Siana moved closer to Snowy. "And rest assured. None of our kind shall ever harm you. And so, farewell."

And suddenly the wolves were gone, and the squirrels looked around them. The cave seemed to be just a normal cave, with a well of fresh water in its centre.

"It is done," said Sammy. "We can leave now."

They emerged from the darkness of the cave, and found it was already early evening, and the light was fading.

Bramble, despite his tiredness, had one more task to perform, and he took off, promising to re-join them back at the Glade.

The squirrels darted up the nearest tree, and began to make their way homewards. They had only gone a short distance when they stopped to watch a remarkable sight. A huge colony of bats, darker than the skies around them, and so fast the eye could not make out individuals, streamed back into the cave, which was now free of restless spirits.

The hidden cave would once again become their shelter and protection through the long winter months.

Sammy, Mrs. Squirrel, Slippy and Snowy were almost home. Fortunately, the rain had all but ceased, and the storm had moved further away.

They reached their camp in the Glade, and Sammy was most pleased that the large drey was dry inside despite the heavy rain – the roof covering had worked marvellously well!

The four squirrels gathered inside the drey and Mrs. Squirrel began to prepare some hazelnut stew. After they had eaten they heard Bramble returning, and they rushed out to greet him. "The bats are in your debt," he said, "and so am I."

"Nonsense," Sammy replied. "There are no debts between friends."

Just as they were about to settle down for the night, and take some well-earned rest, Snowy heard a shuffling noise from outside the drey.

She lifted her head outside and froze in surprise, but then quickly recovered herself and roused the others.

"Come quickly – quickly!" she cried.

The four squirrels leapt out of the drey, and were transfixed by the figure slowly approaching them. It was a fox, a very bedraggled, exhausted and limping fox, who could barely stand. "Oh Felix, Felix!" Mrs. Squirrel gasped, and ran towards him.

"Hello, Mrs Squirrel. I've come for ... a visit." And Felix would have collapsed, if he had not been helped up by the four squirrels who had gathered around him.

*

Shade had found the perfect place to bed down. She had hunted well, and was satisfied. She slid back into the undergrowth, and dug herself in deeply. She was tired, and the cold wind was now piercing. It was time to prepare herself for hibernation, until the warm spring air would awaken her.

For now, she was content to close her eyes, and drift off into a long deep sleep.

Chapter 7: The Tortoise and the Hare

Barnaby the hare let his eyes wander over the fields. The sunlight was starting to fade, but still the rabbits continued to feed. The lookouts were sitting near the entrances to the warrens, every now and again giving a warning thumping on the ground if they thought they spied a predator.

Barnaby had eaten his fill for the day, and was feeling a little weary. He seldom spoke to the rabbits, and was generally quite dismissive of them, being much larger, stronger and faster. He hopped away from the fields, and snuggled down into some warm dry bracken. He yawned, closed his eyes, and it wasn't long before he was in the land of dreams.

*

In his dream Barnaby was having a most peculiar conversation with his neighbours. There was Mr. Squibbles, the rat, old Percy, the wild boar, Mr. Toddle, the tortoise, and a little wood mouse called Squeak. They were discussing a quest to rescue a beautiful princess, who was being held captive by her wicked stepmother in a castle on a hill.

"Now," said Mr. Squibbles, in his most formal voice. "It has come to my attention that the princess is being held in one of the dungeons in the castle. Hanging on a nail, beneath the bars of the prison, there is a silver key to her cell, which the princess cannot reach. Whoever can get to the castle first and free the princess will be rewarded with a sack of gold coins, and live in luxury for the rest of their days."

"I will go and rescue her," said Mr. Toddle.

"You!" Barnaby exclaimed. "You are so slow the princess would die before you ever get there!"

"She will not die!" Mr. Toddle retorted. "And I can reach the castle long before you can, Mr. Barnaby hare!"

Before a real squabble could break out a small voice spoke up. "Please do not argue. I am often made fun of because I am so small," said Squeak. "We cannot help who we are. We are not all made the same, but still, people make fun of us."

There was an awkward silence, and Barnaby couldn't help but feel a little sorry for Squeak, and for what he'd said to Mr. Toddle.

Old Percy shuffled forward. "Allow me to make a suggestion," he said in a deep bass voice. "Let there be a race to rescue the princess, between Barnaby the hare, and Mr. Toddle the tortoise, then we would find out who can get there the quickest – are we all in agreement?" Barnaby and Mr. Toddle both nodded, and so Mr. Squibbles announced:

"The race will commence at dawn tomorrow morning. You will be allowed to bring food for your journey, but no weapons – and you must leave alone, and on foot."

And so, early the next morning, Mr. Toddle and Barnaby made their preparations and were ready to begin the race to the castle. Squeak checked the provisions and nodded to Percy and Mr. Squibbles.

"Very well," said Mr. Squibbles – if you are both ready. "On your marks – get set – go!" And he waved a green flag in the air.

The race had truly begun!

*

Now Barnaby shot off at a rapid pace and was soon a long way ahead of Mr. Toddle. However, it was a very hot day, and the sun was beating down, and he felt that he could afford to take a rest and eat some lunch he had brought with him for the journey. He sat by the side of the road, and after he had eaten, he lay down in the sun to take a nap.

When he opened his eyes Barnaby sat up in surprise, for Mr. Toddle had caught him up and passed him! The tortoise was very slowly making his way along the road and was a little way ahead.

"Well," thought Barnaby, "I must have dozed off for longer than I expected, but no matter, I can easily catch him up and overtake him." And Barnaby jumped up and hopped down the road at a good pace, and was soon a long way ahead of Mr. Toddle again.

A little while later, the road began to get more difficult, narrower and bumpy, and the sun beat down ferociously.

"Ah," thought Barnaby, "I am a long way in front now, and I can see the castle in the distance, so I'll have another rest for a little while."

Barnaby sat down by the roadside, and ate some very tasty carrots he had brought along with him. His eyes felt heavy, and he was a little tired. "I'll just take a short nap," he thought, and soon he had dozed off again.

He woke suddenly, and once more, was amazed to see that Mr. Toddle had overtaken him, clambering slowly down the bumpy road.

Barnaby wasted no time, but bounced up and raced down the road. He soon overtook Mr. Toddle, and was very close to the castle now.

"Just up this hill, and I'll be there," he said to himself.

When he reached the top of the hill he sat down, now feeling very tired. "I'll just stop for a quick break before I rescue the princess," he thought.

And so, he lay down and stretched out, and before long he had fallen sound asleep.

This time when he woke, Barnaby felt certain that he'd only closed his eyes for a few moments, and was confident he was still well ahead of Mr. Toddle, so he sprinted up the hill, knowing he was getting ever closer to the castle.

"Soon all that gold will be mine!" He couldn't help but feel elated. "You'll never catch me now, Mr. Toddle!"

But just when he reached the other side of the hill he saw a sight which made him gasp in disbelief, for up ahead he saw Mr. Toddle taking down the keys of the dungeon and passing them to the princess through the bars of the cell.

A few moments later the princess emerged with a sack of gold coins and handed it over to Mr. Toddle. She then got on a beautiful white stallion and rode off into the forest.

Barnaby stood still, completely dumbfounded. How could this have happened? He scratched his head. "But this is impossible!" he cried.

Suddenly they were all back at the starting line, and Mr. Toddle was being declared the winner by Mr. Squibbles.

"Well done, Mr. Toddle!" said the rat, "and what will you do with all of this gold?"

"Oh, I don't know," Mr. Toddle replied. "I think I will start by going to market and buying some of Farmer Giles' fresh lettuces and pickles. Then I should like to take a long holiday with my good wife, and the rest I shall share out among my family."

There were cheers all around, but Barnaby didn't feel like celebrating. Only little Squeak tried to console him. "Don't feel so bad, Mr. Barnaby," she said. "We can't all be winners."

*

As he slowly walked home, feeling very dejected and confused, Barnaby saw a small red squirrel by the roadside. She was very young, with white streaks in her tail, and a white patch on her forehead. She was too busy foraging to notice Barnaby at first, but as he passed by she looked up at him.

"Hello, Mr. Hare," she greeted him.

"Hello, little squirrel." Barnaby couldn't keep the sorrow out of his voice.

"Why are you so sad today?" asked the squirrel.

Barnaby looked at the ground and didn't want to speak.

"You'll feel better if you tell me," the little squirrel persisted.

So, Barnaby told her the entire story of his race with the tortoise.

"I just can't understand how he beat me in the race," Barnaby concluded, wringing his hands in exasperation.

"Hmm," said the squirrel, with her head tilted to one side. "Mr. Toddle, he mentioned his family – does he have many relatives?"

"Oh yes, he has aunts, uncles, cousins, nephews …"

"Well then," the little squirrel replied, "how do you know it was the same tortoise you saw?"

For several moments Barnaby stood still, and then he clutched his head in his hands.

"Oh, my cabbages and turnips!" he cried. "I've been properly fooled!" And he sat down heavily, and groaned.

The little squirrel shrugged, but before returning to her foraging she turned to Barnaby. "Would you like a hazelnut?" she asked, innocently.

*

Barnaby awoke from his dream, somewhat shakily. He seldom remembered his dreams, but this one had been most odd, and he could recall every detail.

He wondered how long he'd been asleep, and so hopped up to take a look around.

It was early morning, so he must have slept through the entire afternoon and night. He wasn't feeling hungry, but he was thirsty, so he made his way to a nearby stream and took a drink of clear water.

On the way back to his home he noticed a very strange thing. Hanging on a small branch in the middle of a thicket was something that shined and sparkled brightly. Barnaby reached for it and discovered that it was a key – a silver key that glinted in the sunlight …

Chapter 8: Scratch

It was a quiet day in the suburbs, and there was not much traffic around. The road, however, seemed incredibly long and tiresome to Scratch. He walked on aimlessly, and his mind drifted to a conversation he'd had a few days earlier with Smudge, a fellow street-cat, one of his friends from his younger days.

If cats had nine lives then Smudge had about ninety. He had survived motorways, dockyards, council demolitions, numerous gang fights, and worse.

Scratch had run into Smudge in a dirty, narrow alley behind one of the cafés that had recently closed down, and after greeting each other, they began to talk.

"Not much about any more," said Smudge. His voice sounded like an old file being dragged across tough wood.

"No, it's not like the old days," Scratch mused. "Easy pickings and plenty of fun along the way."

"You remember that old place on the corner there?"

Scratch laughed. "Oh, the pub with the chip shop next door – you could always rely on that for a bite to eat!"

"All gone now, Scratch, all gone, and I'm going too – I've decided to move to the big city. It's quite a way, but I think I can make it."

Smudge looked his age. He was half-blind in one eye, partly deaf, and his tail drooped. Scratch didn't think Smudge would last long in the big city, and tried to warn him off.

"But Smudge, it will be dangerous there – more traffic, more humans, and gangs of other cats."

"And more opportunities for food and proper shelter," Smudge replied. "There are many empty buildings and more places to hide. Anyway, I've decided to try it – I'm leaving tomorrow, once I've said goodbye to a few old friends. I'm glad I saw you again. Best of luck to you – you know, Scratch, they say you get older and wiser, but I've found you just get older, and the world gets more confusing."

Scratch had to agree. But if anyone could cope in the big city it would be Smudge. He had a great instinct and capacity for survival.

They said their farewells, and Scratch moved on.

In truth, Scratch had to admit to himself that he was getting slower, and finding things tough going. He no longer enjoyed hunting or chasing other creatures, as it only made him feel more tired. The best part of his day now was having a long snooze in the afternoon, provided he could find somewhere safe to lie down.

The last few winters had been very harsh. He felt the cold more and more with each passing year, and his main priority in winter was to try to stay warm and dry. He also realised he was not as strong as he once was, and in the last few fights he had gotten into with younger cats he had come off worse, which was why one of his ears was now torn, and he walked with a slight limp.

Scratch was thinking about all of these things when suddenly there was a deafening sound in his ears and a huge shape was bearing down on him at an incredible speed. It was almost on top of him when he leapt out of the way at the last moment, and the massive shape roared past him. His nose and mouth were full of fumes and his eyes watered with the putrid smog of burning fuel.

He sat on the path as the truck rattled past, blasting its horn like some demented train that had come off the tracks and couldn't stop.

Scratch realised he'd stepped into the road without thinking, and he was unaware of the truck until it had nearly hit him. This scared him, and he was trembling with shock. He was starting to lose concentration, and his senses were failing him. He tried to calm himself, but every yap of a dog made him jump, every slamming door gave him a start, and the sound of a plane overhead was like a house falling on his head.

Eventually Scratch recovered his wits, and found a wooden bench near a park. He stretched out a little. He was very tired, and soon fell sound asleep.

Sometime later Scratch woke from a nasty dream, and it was then that he realized that it was growing dark, and he was uncertain where he was. He started to move off, but he felt uneasy.

Scratch had, in fact, wandered a little too far, and had ended up lost in an unfriendly neighbourhood. It wasn't long before the other cats appeared. There were at least a dozen of them. At first they only watched him, but soon they were stalking him, circling him, until suddenly they began to chase him, hissing and crying out at him.

Scratch ran and ran. He ran up and down fences, across dangerous roads, through narrow side alleys, and finally, much against his nature, he swam across a stream, which scared him almost as much as being chased. On the other side of the stream he ran on, limping slightly on his front leg, but he had escaped the other cats. Exhausted, he stopped to rest, and after recovering his frayed nerves he began to survey the area warily. He was a long way from the neighbourhood he knew, and now he was in a part of the town he had never seen before. The houses were larger and farther apart, the paths much wider and cleaner than he was used to, and rows of tall trees lined the quiet roadsides.

He was breathing heavily after running for so long, and he looked much the worse for wear. It was cold, and Scratch felt a familiar chill in the air, and knew he must find somewhere to sleep for the night. He was also feeling weak with hunger, as he hadn't had a decent meal for several days, but he was so tired that he didn't have the energy to try to find any food shops or cafes where he might pick up scraps and leftovers. Besides, he didn't have a clue where to start looking.

He tried to clear his head, but he was too weary to think straight. His body was a mass of bruises and cuts, and his eyes were growing heavy. He could only manage a few steps before he crawled under a bush in one of the gardens, and there he fell asleep, totally unaware of the rising wind and pattering rain.

A large storm broke, the wind started to howl and turned bitterly cold. The rain fell down in sheets, saturating the earth, pouring off roofs, and flooding the drains which became clogged up with garbage and filth. But still Scratch slept on, oblivious to all.

*

It was by pure chance that a little girl happened to be looking out of her bedroom window at the storm when she spotted a clump of fur lying under one of the hedges in the garden. She wasn't allowed out after dark, so, as quietly as she could, she crept downstairs, slipped on her waterproof coat and boots, and unchained the lock on the front door. She knew she would be told off, but curiosity got the better of her, and she stepped out into the garden. As she drew nearer to the clump of fur, she could see it was a sleeping cat, very thin and very wet.

The little girl gasped. She was afraid, but she knew she couldn't leave the cat lying out in the rain, so she picked Scratch up and took him into the house.

Now Scratch was used to living on his instincts and wits, and usually when something disturbed his sleep he could sense danger and was immediately alert, but this time things were different. He was simply too tired, so he rolled over and continued to sleep.

The next morning Scratch stretched himself and yawned. He looked about him, before becoming aware that some sort of blanket had been placed over him. It took him some time before he realised he was actually inside a house, and he had never felt this warm before. His immediate instinct was to hide, but when he tried to move he felt soreness and aches all over his body, and besides, he was out of the wind and rain, and yes, a saucer of milk had been placed beside him. Scratch tested the milk once with his nose, before lapping the whole lot up in one go. He had never tasted anything so good.

Before Scratch could decide what to do the door swung open and the young girl came in. An older woman stood behind her, looking uncertain. After seeing that Scratch was awake the young girl went into the kitchen and returned with another saucer of milk and a bowl of food, which she placed before him. This time Scratch didn't even bother to test the food, his hunger took over and he ate ravenously.

When Scratch had finished eating he looked up at the girl, his round eyes shining. The young girl knelt down, and put her hand out to him.

Scratch stumbled towards the girl, but fell over before he could reach her.

The young girl lifted him up, whispered something to him, and laid him down to rest. And there he stayed until the next morning, and many mornings after that.

*

And so, Scratch had at last found a home, and became fond of the young girl. He no longer felt the urge to chase birds and squirrels – he didn't need to – for, at last, somebody had shown some kindness to the lonely stray abandoned as a kitten.

Chapter 9: Underground

Bumble the Badger sat up in his bed, his mind racing, and his heart thumping in terror.

It was the tapping noises again. A distant, hollow tapping, growing nearer and nearer, followed by a weird shuffling noise and horrible dull thuds around the walls of his sett.

At first he thought he was imagining things, overtired and weary when he'd come home at dawn after hunting all night. Perhaps he was just hearing things that weren't there, but then the tapping had persisted, and he was finding it difficult to get any sleep.

The Great Forest itself never slept. At night it became home for many other creatures who hunted in the dark. Owls swooped low, foxes' eyes glittered, and snakes crawled menacingly through the undergrowth, guided to their prey by their uncanny instincts and sharp senses.

Bumble had never really liked the night-time. The stark winter trees scared him, the woods seemed haunted by unknown powers, and the moonlight shone down on strange shapes and grotesque shadows. There were loud snorts and rustlings in the bracken, followed by eerie silences, and Bumble often returned home in fear and trepidation – and then the tapping would begin again.

He considered moving – building another sett – but at this time of year it would be difficult to find the right materials. Besides, it would be a lot of work, and he was tired, and didn't really feel up to it.

For several days the tapping noises stopped, and Bumble lay resting, somewhere between daydreams and sleep.

He was just starting to relax a little, and got out of bed to make some tea, when, with a renewed sense of fear, he started to suspect that some of his belongings had been moved around – and the old bucket he kept in the corner was gone!

Bumble started to panic – what was going on? Had he been burgled while he was out hunting? He did a quick check of his other belongings but nothing else was missing.

This mystery scared Bumble almost as much as the tapping noises. He didn't mind going out in the daytime, so he decided he would take a look outside to see if he could find any clues to these mysteries, so, yawning and weary, he fumbled his way through the long burrows of the underground sett, and scrambled outside to investigate.

The sky was very overcast, and a light rain was falling. At first Bumble wasn't even sure if it was daytime, but a glimmer of sunshine told him it was early morning. He searched through the hedgerows and the undergrowth, but could find nothing amiss. Birds were fluttering around in the tree-tops, and he could hear the distant calls of deer deep in the woods.

Bumble stayed outside for a while, but he soon became tired again, and the rain grew heavier, so he shuffled underground back into his sett – where he was met by an unexpected visitor.

*

Bumble's mother – old Mrs. Badger – didn't visit Bumble very often, and he hadn't seen her for a long time. He kept meaning to visit his parents, but somehow he was always too busy with something else. He felt guilty about this, and knew he should make more of an effort to see them, but old Mrs. Badger didn't seem to mind.

"Oh, Bumble, there you are! I was wondering where you'd got to. But my, you do look thin, have you been eating properly?"

"Oh, yes, I'm fine mother," said Bumble, as he gave her a hug. "I'm sorry I haven't visited lately, but one thing and another …"

"Oh, don't worry about that, your old father is as grumpy as ever!"

Bumble had been named after his father. Old Mr. Bumble was a canny, shrewd, short-tempered old badger who didn't suffer fools gladly. He was a little impatient with his son, considering him to be a dreamer and a drifter, and yet there were moments when he showed great affection towards him.

Old Mr. Bumble was not very popular among the other hedgerow creatures, except in one aspect – he was very good at mending things and making strange new devices. Some of these worked marvellously, like his automatic potato-peeler and his painless tail-clipper, but others, including an incubator for raising self-slicing carrots, sadly didn't work at all. But old Mr. Bumble was never discouraged, or put out. "I knew it would work," he said of his successes, or "It should have worked," he mumbled of his heroic failures.

Mrs. Bumble was long-suffering, but knew it was best not to interfere with her husband's inventions and contraptions – she just sighed and left him to it.

Young Bumble was thinking of his father when his mother interrupted his thoughts.

"You look so tired, Bumble, what have you been doing? – is something wrong?"

"Oh no, mother, I just haven't been sleeping too well, I've had a lot on my mind lately."

"Ah, well, you should eat more, fatten yourself up. It's going to be a long winter, and it's perishing cold outside."

"Yes, yes, I will, mother."

"And no wife and family yet! I don't know – you can't live on your own forever, dear – and all your friends ..."

Bumble sighed, but said nothing.

The truth was, that Bumble had always been a loner. He was happy to keep himself to himself and live by his own rules. He had friends and acquaintances, but the idea of being married and responsible for cubs didn't appeal to his nature, and also frightened him a little. His mother was speaking again:

"Oh, by the way, Bumble. I came to see you a few days ago, but for some reason you weren't in, and this place was such a mess that I tidied up a bit for you."

"Oh!" cried Bumble, and he felt a huge wave of relief wash over him. "So, you moved some of my things?"

"Yes, I took those manky old dishes and cups you left out and gave them a thorough cleaning and put them in the top cupboard. I dusted the furniture and threw out that awful old bucket!"

Bumble was too relieved to tell her that the 'awful old bucket' had been his favourite bucket for collecting soil, twigs, and pieces of wood for repairing the sett.

"Oh mother! I'm so glad you told me – I thought I was going mad, or that I'd been robbed!"

"Don't be so silly dear! Who would steal anything from you?"

And old Mrs. Bumble looked around the place, desperately trying to spot anything that might be worth stealing.

*

Bumble's mother stayed for lunch, and they talked about his younger days and caught up on the family news. Bumble couldn't believe how the years had flown past, and he promised he would visit soon and bring her some fresh peanuts, which had always been her favourite treat.

His mother's visit had explained the mystery of his belongings being moved around, and Bumble felt much happier. He relaxed and went to bed, and soon he was dreaming ...

*

He dreamed of a time long ago, when he was only a cub, and had run away from home. At the time he thought it would be a great adventure, and a chance to escape from continually being told what to do, what to wear, what to eat, and whom he could be friends with.

He resented his parents always interfering with what he wanted to do, so one morning, when they were both sleeping, and his younger brother was visiting their auntie, he sneaked out of the burrow and ran as fast as he could through the thickets and undergrowth. He was full of energy, so he began to investigate the forest.

He wondered at the incredible height of the tallest trees, and the width of the golden lake, where he saw thousands of migratory birds landing and taking off. He saw lizards, as still as statues, basking in the sun, and watched the wasps and bees hum around from flower to flower.

Bumble spent all day out in the open, but by sundown he grew tired and hungry. He thought of returning home, realising that it was getting dark, and soon his parents would be awake and be out looking for him.

Bumble turned uneasily in his sleep.

He realised he didn't know where he was, and a cold panic began to grow inside him. He hadn't meant to run away forever, and he was getting scared as the night-time predators would soon be showing themselves.

But which way was home?

He tried to retrace his steps, but whichever way he went he seemed to go around in circles, ended up back where he had started.

He was lost and alone in the forest, and he could hear the hollow laughter of voices all around him.

"Bumble, Bumble, Bumble! The badger who's afraid of the dark!

Afraid of the dark.

Afraid of the dark.

Bumble, Bumble, Bumble! Always so scared!

Always scared.

Always scared!"

He scrambled and ran, but couldn't get away from the mocking voices. He ran in continuous circles, until he felt he was spinning, dizzily, and from all around him there came a horrible sound, echoing through the Great Forest ...

*

Fear suddenly jolted Bumble awake – he shivered and his eyes were wide open – this time the tapping noises were much louder, much closer, and altogether more terrifying than before.

The hollow tapping and thuds pounded all around the sett, making Bumble's fur stand on end. His teeth were chattering, and his tail was in a quiver.

His terror grew when he realised the tapping had now moved from the walls to the ceiling. He pulled his bedclothes up around him, dreading to look. There was another heavy thud, and then another – and then ... a harsh scraping noise above his head that chilled Bumble to the bone.

He felt paralysed with fear, and couldn't move a muscle.

His nerves were shattered, and he shuddered under the sheets and clung to the side of the bed, waiting for something diabolical to happen – his heart was beating faster, and he knew that every breath could be his last.

He closed his eyes, and whimpered, waiting for the final horror ...

Suddenly the entire roof caved in, with earth, bracken and dust falling all around him.

Bumble snuffled in terror, opened one eye and peeked out above the bed-sheets. A very small, dark, shapeless creature was blinking up at him, blindly, out of the pile of fallen debris.

"Oh dear!" cried the little mole. "So sorry to drop in on you like this – I didn't realize where I was – my name's Molly ... I was tunnelling and seemed to have lost my way."

She had a small little hammer in one hand and a miniature shovel in the other. "This is my first real dig." She bowed her head, looking crestfallen. "I'm afraid I've made an awful mess of things ..."

Chapter 10: Mrs. Squirrel

Mrs. Squirrel was more than happy with her new home in the Glade. She was even happier to see Felix again after all these years.

She had listened intently as he told her of his long journey, and his search for them once he'd reached the forest. After following many false trails Felix had at last picked up a familiar scent and followed it until he had reached the Glade. Felix had been shocked by Mrs. Squirrel's tale of how they had almost lost Snowy at the Rickety Bridge, and had to comfort Mrs. Squirrel as she told the story. He looked upon Bramble with great respect, and they had become good friends, and often went out exploring together, bringing back useful supplies for the small community they were building.

The Glade was more than just a series of dreys and nests for the squirrels now. Bramble had built himself a large roost in the trees, where he often slept during the day, and Felix was working on a permanent den, or 'earth' where he could live, after finding the perfect spot on the far side of the Glade.

There was also a nearby stream, where fresh water was always available, and many forest creatures came to drink there. And so, a community of animals began to visit the squirrels, and friendships were formed. Sammy was so pleased with this that he often invited his neighbours around for a chat, or some berry-wine, and there was a general feeling of contentment among the creatures of the Glade.

Mrs. Squirrel's closest friend was her 'cousin,' Mrs. Rose. They often visited each other, and shared tales of their childhood and memories of the past.

One particular afternoon Mrs. Squirrel was visiting the grey squirrels, as many of them had picked up cuts and bruises from their climbing and foraging, and Mrs. Squirrel had seen them all, applying herbs where necessary to the more serious wounds.

"Mrs. Squirrel," Mrs. Rose announced. "You have remarkable patience with them all, and you do wonders with your healing – and you never complain about them coming to you with their aches and pains."

"Ah, it is no trouble, Mrs. Rose, "I learned healing many years ago, from a wise old squirrel who fixed everybody's ailments, and I would be a very poor cousin if I didn't offer to help."

"Well, I know how grateful we all feel, especially Squirrel Stanley, although he is altogether too grumpy to say so!"

They both laughed, and then Mrs. Rose asked:

"It's strange, but we have been friends for some time, and I don't even know your proper name – it couldn't always have been 'Mrs. Squirrel'."

"No, no, it wasn't – there was a time … oh, but that was long ago, I'm sure you don't want to hear about that."

"But I'd love to hear your story," said Mrs. Rose. "Unless, of course, you'd rather not tell it?"

"Oh, I don't mind telling you my story," said Mrs. Squirrel, "if you really want to hear it."

"Of course I do!" Mrs. Rose replied. "I'll make some tea, and you can tell me the whole tale!"

*

"Once upon a time," Mrs. Squirrel began, for she felt any story worth telling should begin this way –

"Once upon a time, there was a young squirrel who lived with her family near a large town, in a park near a river. She was reasonably content, for she had two brothers and an older sister, as well as her parents, taking care of her.

"The only thing that this young squirrel was unhappy with was her name, for her parents had called her Sessy. Of course, this meant that she was often mocked and made fun of by the other young squirrels, who called her 'Sissy' or 'Silly', which always irritated her. The more she reacted the more the others mocked her, and so she grew up feeling as though she were being laughed at all the time.

"Well, the years passed, and Sessy grew up and thought less about her name than before. Her two brothers had moved away to make their own dreys, and her older sister was soon to be married to a squirrel who lived over the other side of the park, and so they saw less and less of each other.

"Early one morning, before she was properly awake, Sessy's mother came in to see her.

'Sessy, you have a visitor! And look at the state of you – clean yourself up – and hurry!' Sessy resented having to 'clean herself up' to see a visitor, so she made no particular effort, and leaving her fur in a complicated state of disarray, she clambered off her bed, yawned, and went along to see who was asking for her at this unearthly hour of the morning! Her mother had put on that politeness of voice she always used for special visitors, and Sessy heard her say:

'Oh, that's right, just in here – she'll be along in a moment.'

"Sessy snuck around a corner of the drey to get a glimpse of her visitor, but she couldn't quite see, so she turned around to try another way, when suddenly a handsome young squirrel was standing in front of her.

'Hello Sessy,' he said, and his voice was deep and calm. 'I'm Sammy – I live across the park from you – I've brought you something.' And Sammy, somewhat shakily, fumbled in his pockets, and held up a single red rose.

"Sessy said nothing, and made no move. She had never seen Sammy before, but there were many squirrels living in the park.

'I'm starting my own drey soon,' Sammy continued, 'and I was wondering ... if you would like ... to share with me ...?'

"Sessy didn't know what to say – her feet seemed rooted to the spot, as Sammy's round eyes looked into her own. She wondered at the rose which Sammy was holding out to her, and found her hand automatically reaching out to take it.

'Oh my,' she whispered.

"And so Sessy married Sammy, and they moved into a small drey together on the edge of the park. They were very happy that summer, and although the winter was harsh, they never lacked for food, and Sammy worked tirelessly to improve the drey to keep them warmer. By the springtime, Sessy realised she was about to raise a litter of kits.

"Sammy was scampering everywhere, storing up as much food as he could. He was a bundle of nervous energy, and could not sit still. He was constantly asking Sessy if she needed anything, or had enough to eat, until Sessy ordered him out of the drey to go and visit his parents for a while – she needed some peace and quiet!

"One morning Sessy calmly spoke into Sammy's ear. 'Sammy, I think it's time. You better go and fetch old Mrs. Ivy.'

"Sammy fell over himself several times before he found the door, and raced across the field to find Mrs. Ivy.

"Well, it didn't take long – before she knew it Sessy had produced a litter of two kits, a boy and a girl. She was exhausted, but she heard old Mrs. Ivy speaking quietly to Sammy.

'The boy is as strong as an ox, Sammy. He will be a fine young squirrel, but the girl ... I'm worried about her, Sammy. She is so small, and so fragile ... I don't know. You must keep her warm, and give her a little food, but not too much. If she survives the next few days, she has a chance ...'

"Sammy reached over and looked at his two kits. He beamed widely at the boy, who was fast asleep, snoring quietly, and then knelt down and lifted his daughter up.

'Snowy,' whispered Sessy from her bed. 'Her name is Snowy – and the boy, the boy is Slippy.'

"Sammy nodded, and enfolded Snowy in his arms. He sat down in his favourite chair and rocked Snowy gently. He looked up at old Mrs. Ivy.

'I will stay with her,' he spoke softly.

'I'll look in tomorrow," said Mrs. Ivy, trying to keep her voice firm.

'Thank you, Mrs. Ivy,' Sammy replied, and he continued to rock Snowy, wrapping her in his long bushy tail to keep her warm.

"Old Mrs. Ivy left without looking back, so they couldn't see the tears in her eyes.

"The next morning Sessy felt a lot better and was able to sit up. Sammy had fallen asleep in the chair, with little Snowy wrapped in his tail. She was breathing gently.

"A little chirp came from the cot, and Sessy leaned over and picked Slippy up – he was heavy for a kit, and his grip was strong.

"Sometime later Mrs. Ivy arrived. She saw Sammy and Snowy exactly how she'd left them the evening before.

'Sammy, Sammy,' she nudged him awake. 'Let me take a look at her.'

"Sammy gently passed Snowy to Mrs. Ivy. She examined Snowy carefully, and passed her back to Sammy. 'Yes, she's a little stronger,' she smiled. 'You know, Sammy, she just might make it.'

'I know she will,' said Sammy, as Snowy's little fingers lightly gripped his hand.

"For the next few weeks Sammy never left the drey. Food supplies were dwindling, but old Mrs. Ivy brought them some hazelnuts and berries.

'Thank you so much, Mrs. Ivy,' said Sammy. 'I will repay you when the kits are strong.'

'Never mind that,' Mrs. Ivy replied. 'I'm just so happy that Snowy is eating and drinking now.'

'What about these white marks on her tail and forehead?' Sammy asked.

'Oh, they're nothing to worry about – she will always have them, I think. And she will always be small – but she's a tough little cookie!' old Mrs. Ivy smiled.

"One morning, about a week later, Sessy was nursing Snowy, and Sammy was holding Slippy, trying to stop him from wriggling free. Mrs. Ivy was just about to leave.

'You have a wonderful new son and daughter, Mrs. Squirrel!' she exclaimed.

"Just then Snowy's eyes opened. They were large and round and very beautiful, and looked directly into Sessy's.

'Mrs. Squirrel ... love.' Snowy's voice was soft and melodious. And then Snowy closed her eyes, and slept again.

Sessy looked up at Sammy and Mrs. Ivy. Sammy was flabbergasted. He turned to Mrs. Ivy.

'But how ... could she speak? How could she know the words?" Mrs. Ivy looked seriously at Sammy.

'I felt it before, Sammy,' she said, solemnly, 'but I wasn't sure then. I am now. She has the gift, Sammy.'

"Sammy looked over at Sessy, but Sessy was huddling Snowy closely, oblivious to anything else.

"A few days later Sammy returned from his first foraging trip for several weeks.

'Well, Sessy,' he exclaimed. 'I have hazelnuts, walnuts, some delicious pine cones, and red berries! What's wrong, Sessy?'

'Nothing,' Sessy replied. 'But Sammy – I'm not Sessy any more – from now on I'm just Mrs. Squirrel.'

"And every year, on the anniversary of their first meeting, Sammy gave Mrs. Squirrel a young wild rose. And he never once forgot.

*

"And so, that's the story of Sessy Squirrel," Mrs. Squirrel concluded. "Soon after that we moved out of the park and nearer the town, and after several years there we decided to move into the forest – so we made the journey, and here we are!"

Mrs. Rose hugged Mrs. Squirrel and went out to make some more tea. When she came back she said nothing for a while, and they sat together quietly, until Mrs. Rose spoke.

"So Snowy has the gift, Mrs. Squirrel – I've heard of this before, but I've never understood it."

"I don't think anybody does, Mrs. Rose. All I've been told is that every five or six generations there may be one or two kits born with this gift. They can sense many things that the rest of us cannot, and they sometimes know what others are thinking. They can see dreams, and can also feel others' distress and pain, and are often great healers. They instinctively know when the weather is changing, when dangerous storms are approaching, and where to look for food. Some of them can see into the future – or the distant past, and they show wisdom well beyond their years. They are also much faster than the rest of us, and can move almost invisibly – Snowy has some of these qualities, and as she grows up, she is starting to show them more often."

"You must be so proud of her, Mrs. Squirrel."

"She never ceases to amaze me, Mrs. Rose. "Just when I think I understand her she will scamper off and do something extraordinary, but I can't imagine being without her."

Mrs. Rose patted Mrs. Squirrel's hand.

"So, you have no regrets about moving to the forest?"

"Oh no, it's been wonderful – there are dangers, of course, but now we have Felix and Bramble ... they are a tremendous help to us – and more animals are visiting the Glade all the time. I feel quite settled now."

"The winter is never easy," said Mrs. Rose. "The days are growing darker, and the wind is so cold. If it snows it's very difficult to forage for food."

"Yes, but if you grow short of supplies be sure to come to us. We have plenty of food stocked up."

"Thank you, Sess ... I mean, Mrs. Squirrel!"

And they both laughed again.

*

When Mrs. Squirrel reached the Glade she saw Snowy busy digging out some herbs.

"Snowy, stop that for a moment – come over here."

Snowy looked up and scrambled over to Mrs. Squirrel. "What is it mum, is everything all right?"

"Oh yes, everything is fine." And to Snowy's bewilderment, Mrs. Squirrel hugged her close, and whispered, "My little Snowy, my beautiful little Snowy."

Chapter 11: Cassy

The weeks passed by, and the first heavy snow had fallen. An icy wind howled through the trees, and the daylight dwindled quickly. The sky was overcast, and it was getting difficult for the squirrels to forage for food. They often stayed in the warmth of the drey, and only ventured out when there was a break in the weather, and then they would all scurry around, trying to replenish their supplies.

Snowy had seen snow-showers before, but nothing like this, and she was very excited. Early one morning, Slippy found her rolling around in the snow, squeaking and crying out with glee.

"Oh, Slippy, isn't it marvellous!"

"Only if you want to catch your death of cold!" Slippy replied, not sharing her enthusiasm, as he shivered in his thick coat.

"Oh, don't be so boring!" cried Snowy, and she rolled up a large snowball and threw it at Slippy. Slippy was too slow to move out of the way, and the snowball hit him full on the nose. Snowy giggled at him.

"Right! I'll get you for that!" Slippy hurriedly made a snowball and hurled it at her, but Snowy was much too quick and side-stepped it easily.

"Bet you can't catch me!" Snowy laughed, and she threw another snowball at Slippy, which hit him on the ear, and then she leapt up a conifer tree, giggling all the time.

"Right, that's it!" Slippy was getting annoyed as he wiped the snow from his face – I'm going to get you!" And Slippy chased her up the tree, and through the branches of several others.

This went on for some time, until Snowy climbed down, and stopped running. She sat on a pile of snow and waited for Slippy. She was trying her best to look innocent.

Slippy caught up with her and threw a snowball. This time Snowy let it hit her face, and then she started giggling again.

"Oh, Slippy, that was fun!" she exclaimed.

Slippy could never stay angry with her for long, and so he sat down beside her and before long he was laughing too – it had been fun, and he was much warmer now.

From out of the drey, Mrs. Squirrel was suddenly bearing down upon them.

"Look at the state of you two! Slippy, I expected you to show some sense – and you, Snowy – what am I to do with you? Now, get back inside in the warm. Go on – it's freezing out here!"

Just as they were about to return to the drey, Felix emerged from his den. He would usually be sleeping at this time, and he looked very tired and anxious.

"Felix, what's the matter?" asked Mrs. Squirrel, looking concerned.

"A terrible dream, Mrs. Squirrel. A dream of pain and anguish. I think it might be another fox, somewhere in the forest."

"Can you remember the dream, Felix – remember where the other fox is?"

"No, nothing certain, except that it is a long way from here – and the other fox is very weak and cannot move."

Snowy approached Felix. "Close your eyes, Felix. Try to relax, and show me your dream." Felix settled down as if he were resting, and Snowy held onto his hands and concentrated.

Nothing happened for a while, until Felix's breathing began to calm, and then Snowy felt something. It was as if her mind was opening, and she was looking into Felix's memories. Several images flashed before her – images from long ago, some sad, some horrible, and some of happiness, and now – the recent images from his dream. They were very faint at first, but gradually became clearer, until Snowy let go of his hands, and turned to Slippy and Mrs. Squirrel.

"It is a vixen fox, she is caught in a trap. I don't know where exactly, but I have an idea. It is on the edge of the forest. I can see a large clearing – we have to rouse the others – we must hurry, mother – she will die if we do not reach her today."

Mrs. Squirrel looked around at Felix, who was shivering with cold and fear. His eyes were bright and moist.

"We will find her," she said. "Felix, go and wake Bramble. Tell him what's happened. Ask him if he will help us search – Slippy and Snowy, gather some provisions – I'll go and fetch Sammy."

*

And so, the four squirrels, with Felix and Bramble, set off to rescue the vixen. A short while later the snow stopped falling and a mist began to descend in the canopy of the trees. Snowy was a long way ahead, and only Bramble, flying low and silent, could keep up with her. They stopped to let the others catch up. Slippy was astonished as he saw Snowy calmly sitting on a branch. He was aching all over, and quite worn out, but Snowy showed no sign of tiredness.

"How can you move so fast? I can barely see the trees in this mist."

"I don't really see them," said Snowy. "I just know where they are – I can sense them around me."

Slippy shook his head, and looked at Bramble, who had perched in a gnarled ash tree, but the owl remained silent. Sammy and Mrs. Squirrel had caught up by now, and they waited for Felix, who was finding it hard going with the snow underfoot.

"I can't see much in this mist up here," said Sammy. "I think we are close now, and we don't want to miss her. We'll go with Felix from here."

They scurried down the trees, and Felix joined them. He was pawing at the hard ground beneath the snow.

"Anything, Felix?" asked Sammy.

"A faint scent," Felix replied. "This way."

"You need to rest, Felix."

"Not until we've found her, Sammy."

They followed Felix through the outskirts of the forest. The trees thinned out, and by a small brook Felix hesitated, and stopped.

"I can't get a clear scent, but we are close," he said, in a very agitated voice.

He lifted his head and barked as loudly as he could. For several long moments there was no answer, and then, from a clearing up ahead, a faint bark could be heard. "Over here! Quickly!" Felix shouted, and ran towards the cry.

They all leapt after him, Felix barking out, until they saw a young vixen. She was lying down near a hedgerow. One of her front legs had been caught in a spring-loaded animal trap. Blood was oozing from her wound, and her breathing was shallow.

"Oh no!" cried Felix, and he began to claw and snap desperately at the trap, but he couldn't open it.

"Please, Felix, let us try," said Mrs. Squirrel, calmly.

Sammy gently pulled Felix away, while Mrs. Squirrel took the vixen's head in her lap and called to Slippy. "Herbs in my bag, Slippy – and fresh linen."

Sammy and Snowy examined the trap while Slippy fetched the herbs. Mrs. Squirrel began to crush them together to make a salve. At the same time she was speaking gently to the young vixen.

Felix paced up and down in distress.

"Felix, come and talk to her – gently – we must keep her awake." Mrs. Squirrel worked on the young vixen's other wounds – she had been running hard through the forest, and she was covered in nasty-looking scratches and bruises.

Felix controlled his fear and anguish and rested his face next to the vixen's, speaking to her softly, even though she could barely hear him.

"It will be all right. You are with friends now. I promise we will free you."

Sammy looked at Snowy. "What do you think?"

Snowy spoke up. "Bramble, please – we're going to need your help. We need you to pull this piece of the trap back with your talons, while we try to free her leg and pull it clear."

Snowy pointed to where the teeth of the trap had clasped the vixen's leg. It was a vicious-looking contraption, and it would be very difficult to prise open.

"I'll try," Bramble nodded, "but we will have to do it in unison, so, I'll count to three."

Sammy and Snowy took hold of the vixen's leg.

Bramble clutched the trap in his talons and shouted out:

"One, two … three!" and he pulled for all he was worth. Slowly, very slowly, the trap began to open – Bramble was struggling, using all his weight and strength to pull at the trap.

"Get ready!" cried Sammy. "Now!"

With one last effort from Bramble the trap had just opened enough for Sammy and Snowy to pull the vixen's foot clear, and then they heard the trap snap back with a menacing clash of metal – but they were just in time to free the vixen's leg.

"Don't let her fall asleep, Felix!" cried Mrs. Squirrel. "Slippy, the linen – in the bottom of the bag!"

Mrs. Squirrel examined the vixen's leg, feeling along the bones and joints.

"She is badly wounded, but the leg is not broken – she will live if we can get her somewhere warm, and I can treat her properly."

Snowy jumped up. "I will go and have a look around."

"Be careful, Snowy," Sammy whispered.

While Snowy was gone, Mrs. Squirrel tore off some linen and started to wrap it around the young vixen's leg.

"What is your name?" Mrs. Squirrel asked the vixen.

"I am called Cassy," the vixen replied, weakly. "I was drinking at the stream when I heard some humans, so I ran as fast as I could before they could set the hounds on me. I managed to get away before they saw me, but then I stepped into the trap."

Snowy returned, and pointed.

"There is a place, some disused stables, quite close by. It looks deserted, but I can't be sure. There is warm hay and some old blankets inside."

"Good," said Sammy. "We can rest there for a while, until Cassy is able to journey back to the Glade with us."

It took a long time, but with Felix to lean on, Cassy was able to hobble to the stables. The door was not locked, but swung to and fro in the breeze. When they were all inside, Sammy wedged a large stone under the door to stop it from creaking on its hinges.

The animals chose their place to bed down for the night, and soon they were all sound asleep, exhausted by the day's efforts.

*

Three mornings later there was a scuffling noise by the door, and a small hedgehog entered and started to speak.

"Hello, I'm called Heather. I've come to warn you that you cannot stay here. There is a farm nearby, and an old gamekeeper who comes here every so often to check the stores. He has a cottage, just beyond the woods. If he finds you in here he will shoot you all."

"Very well," said Sammy. "Thank you, Heather, we appreciate the warning. Cassy, can you walk?"

"Yes Sammy, I can hobble along."

Sammy offered Heather a reward of some of their food supplies, but she refused.

"You helped our people once, a long time ago, and we do not forget, Sammy Squirrel."

Sammy searched his memory but couldn't think of any time he'd helped the hedgehogs, but then suddenly it came to him.

"Oh yes," he thought, "but that was years ago."

"Thank you again," Sammy said out loud. "And now we must prepare to leave."

The animals could not move very quickly, for Cassy could only manage a slow limp, and the ground was still difficult to walk on through the hard frost. It was a dry, cold, and crisp day, but at least it had stopped snowing, and the wind had calmed down.

The problem was, they were not sure which direction to travel. Even Snowy was uncertain, and it was too misty for Bramble to see much overhead. They started off, tentatively, until Snowy said. "I think it is the other direction." But by then it was too late. They had trespassed into the back yard of the old gamekeeper's cottage.

A low hedgerow ran around the yard, and the animals stopped to wait – all except Sammy, Slippy and Snowy, who had wandered into the middle of the yard. It was just at that moment when the old gamekeeper opened the back door of his cottage and walked out, carrying his shotgun.

*

The sky darkened, and a drizzly rain began to fall. The old gamekeeper saw three squirrels and immediately raised his shotgun.

Mrs. Squirrel tried to run to her family, but Felix held her back.

Sammy ushered Slippy and Snowy behind him and stepped forward. He ignored the shotgun and looked directly at the gamekeeper. The old man took aim carefully. He had shot so many creatures in his life, from deer to rabbits, stoats, hares, foxes and birds, but for some reason, he felt uneasy.

Suddenly his wife appeared in the doorway, wearing a hand knitted shawl and a clean apron. She gasped when she saw the squirrels, and her husband about to fire the shotgun.

For the first time in his life, the old gamekeeper hesitated.

His finger was on the trigger.

Sammy didn't blink.

Felix held his breath.

Bramble knew it was too late to intervene.

Everybody waited for the shot to ring out ...

But it didn't.

The rifle shook in the old man's hands.

The silence stretched out.

Sammy hadn't moved, but stood in front of his children. After what seemed like an eternity, the old man lowered the shotgun.

The gamekeeper's wife ran to him, and put her arms around him. She helped him back into the cottage, as the old man threw the shotgun aside and shook his head, mumbling under his breath.

Sammy took Slippy and Snowy by the hand, and led them out of the yard.

*

The animals watched Sammy in awe as they passed by. The birds were quiet in the trees. Even Mrs. Squirrel was speechless. They followed Sammy back to the stables.

Sammy turned to them all.

"We'll stay here for the night. We'll be safe enough until tomorrow, at least."

Later that night, when the others were asleep, Sammy couldn't stop shaking, and there were tears in his eyes. Mrs. Squirrel held his hands.

"You were so brave, Sammy Squirrel."

"I was terrified," Sammy stammered, "but it was too late to run – what else could I do?"

Mrs. Squirrel didn't answer, she only hugged Sammy closely, until they both fell sound asleep in the warm dry hay.

Chapter 12: Home

Sammy peered through the dusty window of the stables. It was almost dawn. Most of the snow had cleared, and it was going to be a warmer, brighter day. Felix asked Sammy what his plans were.

"Well," said Sammy, "Bramble has been out to see where we are, now it is not so misty, and reports that we are on the edge of the Great Forest, near to the coast, so before we leave I'd like to take the children and Mrs. Squirrel to see something."

"Ah," said Felix. "I think I know what you have in mind – I have seen it, Sammy, and it's not something you easily forget. I will return to the Glade with Cassy. Bramble can come with us, and we'll see you back there later."

"How is Cassy, Felix?"

"I think her leg is nearly mended, Sammy. She seems much better now."

"That's good, Felix, I'm glad we got to her in time."

"Oh yes, I forgot to mention," said Felix, grinning. "I spoke to Mr. Quirk, Sammy, and he asked me to tell you that you are a rogue!"

"Oh, Mr. Quirk" – Sammy's ears twitched. "Well, I did warn him not to climb up that ladder ..."

Felix laughed. "Now that's a story I'd like to hear!"

"You'd have to get several berry-wines into me before I tell you that one!" Sammy chortled. "It was quite a wild caper, Felix."

"Well, I don't know what to say," Felix grew serious. "You've saved my life twice, Sammy – once when I was a cub, and then ... the other time. And now you and the others have saved Cassy – how can I ever repay you?"

"Don't be silly, Felix," Sammy responded. "We would have done the same for any creature in distress – we have a duty to help each other." Felix was silent, but Sammy continued. "Stay with us, Felix, you and Cassy – raise your cubs in the Glade, it is a good place."

"Oh, I don't know if she'll wish to stay with me, Sammy ..."

"Of course she will! Where could she find a braver fox than you, Felix?"

Felix looked abashed, but his eyes were full of hope.

*

The rest of the morning was spent preparing for their journeys, and eating the remainder of their supplies. Just as they were about to depart Snowy pointed up at the sky.

"Father! Mother! Bramble ..."

"Oh my!" Mrs. Squirrel was astounded. "Just look at them!"

Bramble was impressive in flight, but this was something miraculous. The huge birds simply glided effortlessly on the currents of the air, and called out to every creature that they were the masters. Bramble lowered his head as they soared above them.

"They are the emperors of the skies – of all flying creatures," he said. "They are golden eagles."

*

Felix, Cassy and Bramble left for the Glade, and Sammy called his family to him.

"Are we not going back with the others?" asked Slippy.

"Not yet, there's something I want you all to see."

After gathering some supplies they left the warmth of the stables, leapt up into the trees, and made their way deeper into the woodlands. Once in the trees Sammy was much surer of himself. "This is the way," he said. "Follow me, it's not far."

Before long they descended to the ground again and Sammy led them through the thickets towards some large craggy rocks.

"Here, this should do," said Sammy, "climb up."

Mrs Squirrel scampered up beside Sammy. Slippy looked at Snowy and shrugged. "Come on, little sister."

They clambered up the rocks, and when they reached the top to join their parents, Slippy let out a gasp of pure wonder. Snowy stood still, completely lost for any words. Before them was a long narrow beach of pebbles and sand, and stretching out as far as they could see, was the profound and ancient beauty of the ocean.

*

They sat quietly for a long time, watching the waves rolling and crashing below. Suddenly they spied a small boat. It was heading towards an isolated coastal town they could see in the distance. As the boat drew nearer they could see large shapes in the water, and Slippy shouted. "Father! Father! There are huge fish chasing the boats!"

Sammy smiled. "They are not fish, Slippy, they are dolphins. They often follow the boats in and out of harbour. They can jump clear out of the water, and they hunt in packs. They are amazing creatures, playful, intelligent, and yet formidable predators. We are very lucky to see them."

"They are beautiful, father," Snowy whispered. "So beautiful."

*

A short while later, as the daylight began to fade, the squirrels could see many lights come on in the distance, flashes of smoke, explosions, and patterns of light in the sky.

"Father, something is happening in the town," Slippy exclaimed. "The houses are all lit up."

"The humans are celebrating," Sammy explained. "The flashes in the sky, and the colours – they are fireworks. It is the custom of the humans here to celebrate at this time of the year. They stop working, feast, and make merry – they call it 'Christmas.'"

"But father, what are they celebrating?"

"Life," Sammy replied, and held his children close to him.

*

They watched the fireworks light up the sky, and several small boats enter the harbour, but it was growing darker, and it was time to leave.

Sammy Squirrel beamed at his family.

"We've seen many wonders today," he said. "Wonders we will never forget – and now, now let's go home!"

Milton Keynes UK
Ingram Content Group UK Ltd.
UKHW050714300723
425974UK00011B/161